SINISTER

MICHAELLA DIETER

SINISTER

Cover design: 3Crows Author Services
Interior Design: Michaella Dieter
Proofreading: Dee's Notes Editing Services
Editing & Formatting: Michaella Dieter

ALSO BY MICHAELLA DIETER

BEFORE YOU READ

Sinister is a dark forbidden MF romance with horror themes. It contains scenes some readers may find distressing.

These themes include: Graphic murder & torture, graphic sex scenes, graphic language, violence, child abuse (all forms, off-page), starvation, mentions of cancer, kidnapping, and imprisonment.

Please note: *Sinister* was previously published in the *Bad For Me* anthology.

CHAPTER ONE
SINCLAIR

Fourteen Years Ago

"Sin? I'm hungry," my foster sister, Wren, whispers. Her dirty toes flex on the cold tile floor as she peers up at me with large blue eyes that are too big for her tiny face. Her stomach rumbles, emphasizing her words.

We're both hungry. Always eternally hungry, and not just for food. For water, for sunlight, for affection, for warmth. Things I know exist, but having been denied them for so long, it sometimes seems as if the outside world is a dream my fevered mind made up.

Three years we've languished in this run-down fortress buried deep in the forest. Three years since we've seen the stars or felt the warmth of the sun on our face. At eight years old, I'm not sure if Wren even remembers anything before here. If she does, she never talks about it. She stays glued to my side, even when I need to take a piss.

"I know, little bird. I am too." I pull her into my side,

clenching my jaw at the way her ribs poke through the thread-bare dress she wears.

Our foster father, Richard Norris, left two days ago with strict instructions to remain in what used to be a walk-in freezer. He was thoughtful enough to leave two bottles of water, one thin pillow, and a blanket with enough holes in it to make it unworthy of being called such.

Asshole didn't leave any food. It shouldn't surprise me anymore, but I can't help the incredulity. How can you leave two kids behind for days without a scrap of food? The worst thing is, I know he keeps the kitchen well-stocked. Limp Dick, as I secretly call him, goes into town twice a month in his rust-covered truck to bring back supplies. Unluckily for us, he only provides enough to keep us alive, and no more.

He hoards food like squirrels do nuts. He counts the number of crackers in their box, how many blueberries in a punnet. My eyes fall closed at the thought of the ripe fruit bursting on my tongue. *Fuck.* I can almost taste the sweetness, feel the juices running down my parched throat.

When was the last time our bellies were full? A dull ache blooms in my chest at the memories of Thanksgiving dinner. Happy chatter echoes in my mind. Glowing candles, the scent of turkey and stuffing, the clinking of wine glasses. My parents...

I tear my thoughts away from them. They're long gone now, their bullet-sprayed bodies laid to rest in the cold earth. Wren is my family now, and it's my job to protect her. Fuck Limp Dick and his rules. I won't let her go one more day with an empty belly. I can take whatever punishment he dishes out. At fourteen, I'm not as small as I was when I first came here. I can take a few blows if it means Wren goes to sleep tonight with a full stomach.

My legs wobble under me as I force myself to my feet. Waves of hunger and nausea make me stumble, but I clamp them down and help Wren stand. She places her tiny hand in mine, trusting I'll keep her safe. That I'll look after her.

"Stay quiet," I say, and she nods, her gaze fixed intently on the metal door.

I doubt Richard has come back yet, but the insulation in the freezer means I might not have heard him. Blowing out a deep breath, I wrap my hands around the handle and ease it open before sticking my head out and listening. Thick cloying silence greets me, but Richard likes to play games. It could be a trap. Wren's stomach rumbles again, making the decision for me.

My hand tightens around hers, and we slip out of the freezer, hugging the wall that leads to the kitchen. We barely notice the rat sniffing through piles of years-old garbage left to rot, or the thick strips of paint peeling off the walls. The rancid air reeks of mold and decay, promising to kill us with deadly spores before Richard can starve us to death.

It's rumored this was once a fortified home built by an eccentric millionaire convinced there would one day be a zombie apocalypse. Or a nuclear war. Or that the aliens watching our planet would finally have enough of our mistreatment of it. The twelve-foot thick walls envelop the fortress, designed to keep the occupants inside safe. Or, in our case, prisoners.

It was abandoned long ago, left to rot and decay as the surrounding forest takes back what was stolen from it. If only it would also reclaim Arcadia City. It's a cesspool of sin and depravity, a place where corruption runs wild and cops look the other way. Anyone who calls Las Vegas "Sin City" has never been here.

Where else could a man like Richard foster children? Who in their right mind would hand over an innocent like Wren to a monster? And the question I've never been able to answer: what does he want with us? It's been on my mind more and more lately. Is it solely enjoying having power over people weaker than him? Or are we merely pawns being moved around a board in a game we don't know we're playing?

I hate being in the dark. Even as a small child, I had to know and understand what was going on around me. The usual adult response of "We'll tell you when you're older" never flew with me. So being kept in a perpetual limbo is my own personal hell. It's another way for Limp Dick to torture me.

We round the corner and push through the swinging doors into the kitchen. Unlike the rooms we're restricted to, Richard keeps his cleaner. He won't subject himself to the filth he forces us to live in.

The stainless-steel refrigerator hums in the corner, and I fall on it like a wolf with its prey. I toss cooked drumsticks, a block of cheese, a package of ham, and a punnet of the blueberries I've been dreaming of onto the counter. Wren watches me with wide eyes, her arms wrapped defensively around her middle.

I laugh and scoop her up, settling her on the counter next to the food. "Eat, little bird, as much as you can before Richard comes back." I tear off the Tupperware lid and hand her a drumstick. Her tongue darts out to wet her lips before she tears into it like a starving animal.

It's what he's reduced us to. Animals. He's stripped us of almost everything that makes us human and brought out the feral, instinctual parts of us normally buried deep inside.

I tear off a chunk of cheese and break it in half, giving one to Wren before stuffing my mouth with the other. Spying a baguette on the opposite counter, I stalk over and grab it, biting into the doughy goodness with a groan. Wren scoops berries into her mouth, the juices dribbling down her chin while her legs swing back and forth, her heels thudding against the wooden cupboards.

The doors crash open with a bang, and Richard's angry yell sends ice running through my veins. I snatch Wren off the counter and hold her to my chest as I back away from the seething monster, a cold sweat dotting my forehead.

Richard advances toward us, his dark-blond hair standing on end while his eyes spit daggers. "I'm sure I remember telling you to stay in the freezer," he says, his voice dangerously soft. "In fact, I'm positive. Now, I find you in my kitchen, eating my food. I'm very disappointed in you, Sinclair. I thought you knew the rules by now."

"I couldn't let Wren—" His fist smashes into my nose, making me stagger back. Blood rushes into my mouth, the metallic tang heavy on my tongue. Wren screeches and tightens her hold around my neck, and my arms band tighter around her. I turn my back on Richard—a dangerous move—but I have to protect Wren from his fists.

Heavy blows land on my back and over my kidneys, making the breath leave my lungs. I murmur nonsense into Wren's ear to calm her, but it doesn't work. Her heart hammers against mine, while her panicked breaths ruffle my hair.

"Take her away," Richard bellows, and I risk peeking over my shoulder. Five men I've never seen before barrel into the room and advance toward me.

"No!" I shout, backing away. "Leave her alone. Take me."

Richard's face morphs into a vicious sneer. "I have no use for disobedient children." His gaze flicks toward the men. "Dispose of her body in the woods. You have my permission to play with her first."

My heart tears in two as the men descend on me, ripping Wren from my iron grip. My fist rears back and connects with the man holding Wren, but Richard yanks me away. I shout Wren's name, fighting Richard's hold. I'm not strong enough. I'm never enough.

Wren screams my name, tears streaming down her face, her thin arms reaching for me as they carry her out of the kitchen.

I stamp on Richard's foot and tear away from him, but he yanks me back by my hair.

"Sinclair!"

I burn Wren's image into my mind, along with the men that took her. The doors swing closed, blocking my view. "I'll kill you for this," I hiss at Richard before everything goes black.

~

A JARRING BOUNCE and rattle pull me from the shadows. Unbearable pain slams into me, taking my breath away. I peel my eyes open and fight the waves of nausea coming from the swaying motion beneath me. It takes a moment for my brain to register that I'm lying in the flatbed of Richard's truck, and that I'm outside for the first time in years.

Dark-gray clouds fill the sky in a roiling mass, echoing the turmoil raging inside me. Lazy fat raindrops ping against the rusted metal surrounding me, and I open my mouth, hoping I might catch one or two to help clear away the metallic taste of blood on my tongue.

The vehicle swerves, and my neck flops to the side, revealing my arm bent at an unnatural angle. A painful breath hisses from my lips, and deep racking coughs blaze a trail of fire across broken ribs. Limp Dick must have beaten me once I was unconscious. *Coward.*

As the truck continues on its journey, anger and despair rage through me. I watch dispassionately as the trees surrounding the road grow thicker. There's no way of telling how much time has gone by between those bastards taking Wren away and now. I don't know if she's still alive. Why the fuck did I sneak out? A tear leaks out of the corner of my eye, and I press my lips together. Guilt joins the anger and despair while my inner voice berates me for allowing them to take her.

If only I was strong enough. Old enough. Powerful

enough. She was all the family I had left, the last person on this miserable fucking planet I cared for. And I let them tear her from my arms. Her screams and the look of desperation and terror on her face will be with me for however long I have left to live—which probably won't be long. Richard isn't the type to leave witnesses running around, even if this city is morally bankrupt.

The truck lurches to a halt, and I grit my teeth as my broken arm smashes into the side panel. Limp Dick whistles a jaunty tune as he gets out and walks around to the back. He opens the tailgate and stares down at me with a malicious grin before grabbing my ankles and hauling me out.

I clench my jaw, refusing to allow him the satisfaction of my screams. He sets me on my feet, and my body sways as a fresh wave of pain lances through me. I spit in his face, then watch with satisfaction as the fat globule slides down his cheek.

Richard's grin grows wider. He flicks it away, then forces me to move forward. I stumble over my feet, still weak from the beating and starvation. My throat closes when the sound of roaring water reaches me. *No, no, no.* The trees give way to the Aries River, known for its strong current and white-capped waves. He throws me up against the side of the wooden bridge, pushing my back out into the open air.

I grab hold of his jacket, using the last bit of strength I have left to try to save myself. The sound of the river fades against the frantic beat of my heart. Richard leans forward, pressing his body against mine, and I flinch when his hard dick digs into me.

"My men informed me that Wren was a tasty little treat. They enjoyed her before strangling her and burying her used-up body in the woods." He rubs his groin against me, and bile rushes up my throat. "I had such plans for the two of you. Too bad."

He peels my fingers from his jacket and shoves me. The

world turns over and upside down as my body soars over the bridge, and images slam into my skull.

Scoring the winning soccer goal, my parents jumping up and down, shouting with pride. Opening presents on Christmas morning beside a roaring fire. My mom teaching me how to dance, because even if girls were icky, one day, they wouldn't be. The sound of the gunfire which ripped them away from me. Meeting Wren and vowing to protect her. Wren being torn from my arms with tears streaming down her face.

"They enjoyed her before strangling her and burying her *used-up body in the woods.*" The words replay in my mind as my battered body hits the river with a painful smack before sinking. A wreath of bubbles surrounds me, tickling my face in greeting before dissipating. The current carries me away from the bridge, and I peer up through the murky water, seeing the wavering outline of Richard's truck speeding off.

My lungs burn as the last of the oxygen bubbles from my lips. Panic vanishes as a sense of peace envelops me, a sort of euphoria that I reach out and hold tight to. Maybe I'll see my parents and Wren again. *There's no use fighting, just let go.* My eyes close, and a small smile curls my lips. Just as the darkness seeps around my consciousness, my body slams into the bluff edging the river. My eyes fly open as thick roots jutting into the water scrape against my body.

You failed to protect her. You broke your promise. Are you really going to give up? Let them get away with it? The thoughts punch into me, and a final shred of determination gives me enough strength to grab on to the roots with my good arm. I hold tight and lift my head out of the water, my lungs seizing as precious air fills them. Deep coughs rack my body, threatening to send me back into the river.

"Here, lad, take my hand." The grumbly voice startles me, and I almost lose my precarious grip. An older man, perhaps in his fifties, leans over the bluff, his hand thrust out toward me.

"My-my arm's broken," I gasp out, still choking on water.

8

The man cocks his head. "So you're going back into the Aries, then? That's a disappointment." He settles back on his haunches and looks at me with a raised brow. "Go on. If you don't want to live, just give up."

I clench my teeth. Wren's ghost appears before me, her enormous eyes pleading with me. I blow out a breath and sling my broken arm up, swallowing down the scream that so desperately wants to be released. The man grabs my wrist and hauls me up, dropping me to the muddy ground once I'm clear.

"What's your name, lad?"

I lie in the wet mud, shuddering through the fiery pain lighting up my nerves. What is my name? Sinclair West went into the river and died beneath the white-capped waves. I slam my hands into the earth and push myself up, meeting his eyes.

"My name is Sinister."

CHAPTER TWO
SINISTER

Now

The disheveled man glares at me with a defiant glint in his eye. I chuckle, a dark and foreboding sound that would send most fleeing in terror. The citizens of Arcadia City whisper my name, afraid to invoke The Carver. Parents use me to keep their children in line—a boogeyman of sorts. *Go to bed, Timmy, or Sinister will come.*

As if I would ever hurt a child.

This piece of shit in front of me, though? He's another story. It's been fourteen years since I last laid eyes on him. He was the one to take my sister from me, and now, he's going to tell me where Limp Dick's hidey-hole is. He went off the grid about a year after I pulled myself out of the river, and there have been very few sightings since.

I can't wait to come face-to-face with the monster of my youth.

"Most men wouldn't dare look at me with such disrespect," I murmur, spinning my knife between my fingers.

"Especially not while hanging naked from the ceiling in chains."

"Fuck you, Sinister. I ain't telling you nothing."

The corner of my mouth lifts. "You know who I am."

"All of Arcadia knows who you are. The Carver, Aidan O'Brien's lackey." His blue eyes flick over my large frame and dismiss me like I'm nothing special. "A glorified lapdog that heels when his master calls."

I hum and move closer to him. Sweat glistens on his brow, giving away his fear. I'll give him credit; he hides it well. It's a testament to his loyalty to Richard—usually by the time my shadow crosses their door, they're on their knees, spilling their secrets before I so much as lift a finger.

"Is that the only way you know me, Jacky boy?" I ask, running the flat blade down his chest. "By my reputation?"

Jack leans back, the whites of his eyes showing. He struggles against the chains spreading his arms and legs out wide, like Leonardo da Vinci's Vitruvian Man. It seems Jack can only hold on to his mask of bravado for so long. I wonder how much longer—and what I'll have to resort to—before he begs me for mercy.

I have none. Not anymore.

"Let me refresh your memory," I say when he doesn't answer my question. "Think back. Fourteen years ago, you stormed into a fortress in the woods. You ripped a young girl out of a boy's arms. You defiled her, strangled her, and left her body alone in the cold."

The acrid stench of ammonia hits me when Jack's bladder releases. Ah, there it is. Now he knows why he's here, and the knowledge he won't walk out of here alive makes him slump in the chains.

"There, there, Jacky. All you have to do is tell me where Richard is. No, wait. I also want the location of my sister's grave. She deserves a proper burial, doesn't she?"

Jack shakes his head. "You're going to kill me anyway. I'm not telling you anything."

A vicious smile splits my face. "I was hoping you'd say that." I kneel at his feet, uncaring that my black pants soak up Jack's piss. I take his foot in my hand and run a finger down the top. He jerks and tries to pull it out of my grasp, but my fingers tighten around it. "I like to start from the bottom," I say while gliding my knife around his ankle. "I find it works better that way."

The knife cuts into his skin and circles around his ankle. It splits beautifully, peeling back as I go. I ignore Jack's cries and slide the knife up the back of his calf to his knee and cut another circular mark there. Warm scarlet blood seeps from the cuts, the metallic tang heavy in the air. My mouth waters at the sight, and I hum a nonsensical song as I work.

"Last chance, Jacky boy. Tell me where they are." I raise a brow, but he clenches his teeth. "Okay, then." My fingers dig into the cut along his calf. "Ready? One...two...three." It takes several tugs, but his skin separates from his leg, leaving behind gleaming muscle. His screams pierce the air, bouncing off the walls in a stunning symphony of agony.

I grin up at him, pleased with the noises he makes. "I'm going to do your thigh next, Jack. Unless you're ready to talk?"

"Fu-fuck you," he groans, his fists clenching.

"As you wish."

I repeat the process on his thigh, followed by his other leg. When he passes out, I take a break to admire my work. The human body and all its magnificence has always fascinated me. The intricate webbing of nerves and vessels, the flow of muscles, the hard-working organs determined to keep us alive.

It took me years to develop my techniques, for my knife to become an extension of my body. I wield it much like an artist does their paintbrush, bringing masterpieces of blood to life. It's why they call me The Carver. Unlike butchers, who have no care for how they dismember bodies, I'm more of an artist. Each body is a piece of work I leave my signature on.

When boredom sets in, I push off the wall and wander over to the trolley I prepared earlier. There's no point working on an unconscious body. I dose him with a shot of epinephrine, followed by a special little dose of something The Chemist worked up. He's very picky about naming things, so although he created the serum over a year ago, it still hasn't got a name. But it's fucking magic in a syringe.

When you combine it with epinephrine, it not only speeds up the heart, draws blood away from the skin, and makes your lungs work more efficiently, but it also keeps you conscious, no matter how much pain you're in. And it comes with an additional bonus—it amplifies your pain receptors, making a paper cut feel like an amputation.

Jack won't be able to deny me now. Even if I have to peel every inch of skin off him.

A low moan spills from his lips, quickly replaced by a garbled sound of horror as he looks down to see the desecration of his legs. "Fucking monster," he mutters, his head swinging to the side.

I chuckle and pick up a spray bottle from the trolley. "I'm still waiting, Jack. I won't let you die until you've told me what I want to know."

His back arches, the tendons in his neck standing in relief as a primal scream rips from him. Lemon juice sprayed on open flesh will do that to a man. He writhes and moans, curses me and any children I might one day have. Why does he persist in fighting? It would all go away if he just told me.

"Where is Richard?" I demand before spraying his left leg. "I can make the pain stop." He shakes his head, and I shrug. I get to work removing the skin from his ass and hips. The magic drug does its job of keeping him awake, and I can only imagine the level of pain he's in. It's got to be off the charts.

"I don't know!" he screams when I hold his flaccid dick in

my hand. My head cocks to the side as I rest my knife along its length. "I haven't seen him in years, okay?"

"Then why would you go through all this to protect him?"

Jack's throat works as he swallows. "It wasn't for him, but for who he works for. If I talk, he'll kill everyone I know."

I purse my lips as I stare at him. It doesn't surprise me to learn Richard was working for someone, but he's the only one I care about. This mystery boss is of no interest to me. I only care about making Richard and the five men who took Wren pay.

But since he's talking... "What did Richard want with us?" No matter how much I've dug over the years, I've never been able to find out.

Jack groans. "There were cameras set up around the fortress. A benefactor was paying for videos of the two of you."

My brow furrows. "Videos of what?" All we did was get beaten and starved.

"That's what the benefactor wanted," he replies. I must have spoken those last words out loud. "He wanted home movies. He wanted to see you abused. Once you and the kid got attached, he was going to force you on her."

Bile rushes up my throat, but I choke it down. "So why did Richard have you kill her instead?"

"I don't know, man. The benefactor died in some freak gas attack in London. Maybe no one else would pay the fees. These guys are very particular about what they want. They give descriptions, and Richard sends us out to match the brief."

A chill runs down my spine, and I take a step back. I want to place my hands over my ears like a child when Jack continues to talk. When he describes how they would hunt at doctor's offices, playgrounds, sporting events, and carnivals. How they would take pictures and the "benefactors" would choose who they wanted. How they would then kill the parents, making the children homeless and at the mercy of corrupt CPS agents.

They murdered my parents due to the whim of some mysterious man behind a screen. All because he wanted me to fulfill his perverted fantasy. For the first time in fourteen years, tears mist my eyes. I swore I would never again be weak. That I would never allow emotions to prevent me from doing what needed to be done.

The corner of Jack's mouth lifts. "But that little girl? Man, she was something else. The way she screamed when we—" I punch him in the face hard enough to snap his head back. He spits blood and chuckles. "She called for you, you know. 'Sinclair! Help!'" he mocks in a falsetto.

Fuck my promise to not let my emotions get the better of me. A crimson mist settles over my vision, my heart rate amps up, and my mind detaches. I close off my ears as I settle deep inside myself, letting The Carver's practiced movements take over.

I start with Jack's dick, severing it at the root before stomping it into the tiled floor, decimating the object that hurt Wren. I dose him up with another injection of The Chemist's serum, watching with a critical eye as the pulse in his neck quickens. Blood gushes from the amputation site, the hot liquid running down his mutilated legs and into the drain strategically placed below the chains.

Jack's mouth opens wide with never-ending screams, but I hear nothing as I swipe my knife over his lower stomach. With the delicacy of a surgeon, I pull the intestines through the slit. There's not much time left; with each pump of his heart, he loses more blood. But I don't want him to go that easily. He's going to feel the same terror Wren did.

I handle the delicate mass in my hands, gently tugging more out until I'm able to drape it around his neck. Once they're in place, I slap Jack's cheek to get his attention. His glazed eyes meet mine, and in them, I see his pain and misery. *Good.*

"This is for my sister," I murmur, and wrap the slippery tubes around my hands. Jack's breathing hitches, his eyes popping wide as I strangle him like he did Wren. His body jerks and thrashes, making the chains rattle merrily with his death dance.

Normally, one of my victims would pass out from the strangulation, but the serum won't allow it. Jack feels every torturous second, every ounce of terror his mind feeds him as it scrambles to live.

One down, little bird.

Satisfaction thrums through me when the light leaves his eyes. He'll never hurt anyone again, and Wren now has a sixth of her revenge. I'll hunt down the others, no matter how long it takes. I won't rest until their blood turns the streets red.

CHAPTER THREE
DOLLY

I sit back, checking my makeup in the mirror with a critical eye. It's a special night, and I'm determined to look my best. *Something's missing.* My head cocks to the side, and I purse my lips, tapping my fingers on the ancient battered dressing table I rescued from the roadside. Ah, yes. Contacts.

Tilting my head back, I stare sightlessly at the industrial HVAC ducts running under the ceiling as I pop in one red-colored contact after the other. They go well with the crimson wash covering my natural brown hair. Tonight, I've gathered it into two low pigtails and tied them off with pink ribbons.

When I'm satisfied, I push off the stool and stalk over to the dented rail I use as a makeshift closet. The poor thing doesn't have much to offer me in the way of clothes, but I sort through each item as if it was new. *No, no, no...yes.* My fingers clutch the hanger, drawing out a pink polka-dot dress with crinoline skirts. The corner of my mouth lifts as I imagine his reaction. Will he love it?

After donning the dress, I draw silk stockings up my legs and tighten the ribbons at the top to ensure they stay in place.

White Mary Janes with flowery broguing along the toecap complete the ensemble.

I do a little spin in front of the cracked full-length mirror and grin at the creepy visage looking back at me. I resemble a demonic doll with my over-rouged cheeks and perfectly drawn bowtie lips.

A little shiver of anticipation slides down my spine when I glance at the clock. Fifteen minutes before he arrives. This is going to be so much fun. He's in for the night of his life.

I slide out of the small bedroom I've made out of the old overseer's office at the back of the warehouse and make my way down the rickety wooden stairs. I'm not sure what the warehouse used to be used for, but it's been abandoned for years, along with many more like it in Arcadia City's docklands.

On clear nights, I often gaze out over the polluted, filthy water and wonder what it must have been like over a hundred years ago when the first settlers came. Did they look at the mighty river, the expansive bay, and deeply forested hills and think they'd found paradise? Is that why they named it after the Greek version?

I scoff. If so, there's nothing left of their utopia. Shallow graves litter the hills while predatory men stalk the streets. The sound of gunfire is so common, no one bats an eyelid. The police force is a joke, each member greedier than the last, easier to buy off than the drugged-up prostitutes forced to work the corners.

Stepping onto the main floor, I sweep my gaze across the warehouse before dragging a false wall across the width to hide my bedroom from prying eyes. I've sectioned the space off into little rooms, like a dollhouse. The living room is my favorite. The worn royal-blue couch with the cat scratches along the side. The threadbare oriental rug with the cigarette burns. The cracked teapot sitting in the middle of the rusted metal coffee table. It's so pretty, so homey.

It's amazing what people throw away. I rescued all my treasures from the landfill or the roadside. My fingers graze the top of the teapot before I turn away with a flounce of skirts and double-check all my rooms are just right for my visitor.

The little cuckoo clock I rescued from a dumpster lets out a broken wheeze, informing me the time has arrived. I dim the lights to a pale glow and stand at the door, bouncing on my toes. Anticipation hums through my veins, and my tongue darts out to wet my lips when three loud raps sound at the door. I straighten my shoulders and throw open the door, offering my visitor a welcoming smile.

"Welcome to The Dollhouse, sir. Please, come in."

The scrawny man with salt-and-pepper hair, gray eyes, and a sallow complexion glances over his shoulder before pushing past me. I peer out into the dark night, sweeping my eyes over the empty parking lot before closing and bolting the door.

"May I take your coat?" I ask, ever the proper hostess. He shrugs out of the black trench coat and hands it over before looking over my ensemble.

"Nice," he says, licking his thick lips. His gaze comes to rest on my chest, where my breasts threaten to spill out of the low neckline. I let out a giggle while I hang up his coat.

"Do you like?" I ask, doing a little twirl. Lust blazes in his eyes, and I offer a coy smile. Mr. Ashton, here, is a CPS agent —one of the most corrupt in Arcadia City. Young girls are his specialty. It's a good thing I appear younger than my age, because he paid five hundred dollars for me, thinking he was going to get easy pussy.

I grab his hand and pull him into The Dollhouse, smiling at him over my shoulder. Not that he'd notice; he's too busy looking at my ass. When we reach the living room, I shove him down on the couch and hand him a chipped teacup.

"Will you have a tea party with me, Mr. Ashton?" I ask. When he nods, I spin away and grab the teapot. His eyes bug out when I bend over, my breasts almost falling in his face.

The fool doesn't even notice the teapot descending toward his head.

"Oopsie," I murmur when he falls back against the couch with a grunt. A thin line of blood trickles from a gash just above his eyebrow. I swipe it away and add it to the other stripes on the wall. Mr. Ashton makes thirteen. My lucky number.

I flick a switch, and the warehouse descends into darkness for a moment before blue lights click on, bathing the rooms with an eerie glow. Words appear on the walls, only visible when the lights come on.

Murderer. Rapist. Abuser. Pedo. Liar. Thief. Adulterer. Bigot. Racist.

Unbeknownst to the men I lure to The Dollhouse with promises of fulfilling their perverted fantasies, I created hidden tunnels inside the walls, allowing me to hunt them without being seen. I need every advantage possible when working against bigger and stronger men.

I duck into one now, hidden behind a broken grandfather clock, and peek through one of the many disguised holes to wait for him to shake off the blow to the head. *Come on, you wuss. I didn't hit you that hard.*

Moments later, Mr. Ashton comes to and pushes himself to the edge of the couch. His head turns back and forth before he stands, wavering on his feet. "Dolly?" He stops short when he notices the words written on the walls before backing away.

I slide down the passageway and collect Barbie. My hands wrap lovingly around the warm wooden handle, like greeting an old friend. She winks back at me in small flashes of light glinting off the razor blades embedded around the top half of the bat.

Long ago, someone told me I had the voice of a fallen angel. I use it now, letting it rise into the air, the melancholy tones echoing through the warehouse's excellent acoustics.

"All around the mulberry bush..." I sing the nursery rhyme

in low tones, drawing out the words to add to the creep factor. *"The monkey chased the weasel."*

The blue lights flicker and dim when I press a button on the wall, creating thick shadows for me to hide in. A vicious grin splits my face when Mr. Ashton stumbles over a chair and falls to the ground with a thud. I race toward him, lifting Barbie above my head.

"The monkey stopped to pull up a sock..." Barbie crashes into his lower back, knocking the breath out of him. Using my foot, I turn him over and cock my head, my grin growing even wider.

"Why are you doing this?" Mr. Ashton forces out between clenched teeth.

I pull a photo of me as a young child out of my pocket and thrust it in his face. It takes a moment for his eyes to focus on it before they widen and his skin pales. "No, please—"

"Pop! goes the weasel." Barbie smashes into Mr. Ashton's jaw, dislocating it and tearing the flesh to shreds. I don't want or need to hear his pathetic excuses.

When my parents died, this piece of shit sold me. During my captivity, they forced me to service the needs of the sick men who wanted me to call them *daddy* or *sir*. They didn't care that I was only a child. In fact, most of them preferred it.

Teachers. Husbands. Fathers. Judges. Lawyers. Priests. I marked each of their faces and committed them to memory. I'll never forgive. Never forget.

I gained my freedom two years ago, and I vowed I'd make every one of them pay. The corruption in Arcadia may run to the highest levels, but I'll take out as many of them as I can. I'm under no illusion I'll ever leave this city alive. One of them will overpower me, and I'll find myself floating in the Aries River or in a shallow grave in the Olympian Hills. Just another statistic.

But that's okay. Because with death will come peace and the end of the nightmares that torment me every night. I'll never have to remember the innocent little girl I once was or relive the tortures forced on me.

"Pop! goes the weasel," I repeat in a whisper, and bring the bat down on Mr. Ashton's face, over and over again, until even his mother wouldn't recognize him. Bits of flesh, bone, and brain matter decorate The Dollhouse and my pretty dress when I'm done, but it's nothing a little bleach can't handle.

CHAPTER FOUR
DOLLY

S itting in a dark corner of the bar, I keep my hood up while listening to the chatter going on around me. Although they would claim otherwise, men are as much gossipers as women. The topics might differ, but the result is the same.

I dredge a french fry in ketchup as I strain to better hear the conversation in the booth to my left. Three men, most likely fishermen by their clothing and the scent of fish hanging over them like an aura, drown their woes in cheap beer and greasy burgers.

"The man was skinned!" the eldest of the three says, thumping his fist on the worn wooden table. He pushes back the royal-blue beanie he wears, revealing shoulder-length hair the color of snow.

"Someone told me he was one of those kiddie diddlers," another one says. I risk a peek in their direction, my lip curling into a sneer. He must sense me, as he tries to peer over his friends' shoulders in my direction, but I put my head back down. Staying invisible is the name of the game.

"Betcha it was Sinister that's done it," the third says, a

portly fellow with sun-damaged skin and heavy lines etched in his brow.

"Shh!" the eldest admonishes. "He has ears everywhere." He lowers his voice, but I can still make out when he adds, "Roddy told me there was an S carved into his back. It was definitely The Carver." The other two nod wisely, as if that explains everything.

I've recently discovered that Sinister and The Carver are the same person. Since moving back to Arcadia City, I've heard his name whispered in both reverence and fear. I haven't been able to glean too much information about the man; it's as if he's a ghost.

But I made a vow to help rid this city of corruption, and my conscience won't allow what appears to be a serial killer to run loose on the streets. The men finish their drinks before tossing a few notes on the table and vacating their seats. I dart a glance around before reaching over the seat and helping myself to the newspaper they left behind.

The Herculean Gazette's stories must always be taken with a pinch of salt. Or better, an entire bucket of salt. Once corruption settles into the heart of a city, it gradually spreads like a fungus. It creeps into every home, every office, every street. It lies dormant, waiting for its opportunity to strike before spreading anarchy, malfeasance, and apathy throughout the population.

The Gazette is no different. The editors print what Governor White wants the people to believe. His specialty is dividing the populace. One week he attacks minorities. The next, the disabled. The following, the poor. It keeps the people in a constant state of hatred and discontent—all to prevent them from looking too closely at what he does behind their backs.

But news is news, even if I can't trust all of it to be truthful. The front-page picture takes up half the page and displays a body bag sitting at the edge of Hera Bay. "Fuck," I whisper as

I scan the article. The body was dumped a mere three hundred yards from my warehouse—far too close for my peace of mind.

The article mentions the S carved into the victim's back but doesn't accuse Sinister directly. They never do—at least in the ones I've read. It hints at him having power or some kind of sway, and that makes me nervous.

Especially if he's dumping bodies in my neighborhood.

Some rumors say he's a vigilante, killing only the most evil of society. Others claim he's nothing more than a hitman for Aidan O'Brien—the head of the local Irish Mafia. And some refute both of these, dismissing him as nothing more than a scapegoat, a convenient fictional character they can blame their crimes on. *No, officer, it wasn't me that killed that man. It was Sinister. See the S?*

How convenient.

I scan the rest of the paper before dropping a twenty on the table and making my way out of the bar. The thick clouds and heightening winds predict rain, so I lower my head and pull my hood tighter over my face before disappearing into Arcadia's streets.

Trying to decide if I should focus on luring another victim to The Dollhouse or searching for more information on Sinister keeps my mind occupied as I weave through downtown. There is a disproportionate number of homeless here, begging outside of businesses. Passersby ignore them for the most part, turning them into nothing more than scenery.

I drop a few dollars into cups here and there. I have little myself, but I like to spread around the money my victims pay me where I can.

After checking both ways for cars, I dash across Styx Avenue and turn right onto Eros Lane. Even though it's only 4 p.m., prostitutes already line the street, dressed in skimpy clothes grossly unsuitable for the weather. At least the street receives a bit of protection from the wind because of the tall buildings lining both sides.

My gaze jumps from one person to another, my heart breaking at how young many of them are. I wish there were more of me, an entire army that could clear the city of corruption and make it new. A place of safety, where kids could play outside and women could walk down the street. But I'm only one person, and I can't solve it all on my own.

"Mary," I murmur, coming to a stop alongside one of the women. She's thinner than she should be and wears a hot-pink miniskirt and matching crop top. Goosebumps cover her arms, blending in with the fingerprint bruises decorating her forearms. She startles, a hand coming to rest over her heart.

"Dolly! You need to stop sneakin' up on people."

My lips turn down. "Sorry. Are you and the others doing okay? You look cold."

Her right shoulder lifts. "Ain't gonna cover up the goods, sugar. There's no money in that."

I slide a fifty-dollar note into her palm. "I was hoping I might pick your brain. What do you know about the man called Sinister?"

"Jesus Christ, girl, keep your voice down. That's not a name you say out loud." She grabs me by the shoulder and hauls me into a nearby alley, glancing wildly over her shoulder.

I lean back against the brick building and cross my legs. An exhaust vent rains heat down on us, and Mary's shoulders relax as the warmth brings back some color to her cheeks. "He's real, then?" I ask, searching her brown eyes. Close up, her age is more apparent. Her cheap box dye doesn't fully cover the grays at her temples, and wrinkles line the edges of her mouth.

Her hands shake as she pulls a ratty box of cigarettes from her purse. After lighting it, she pulls in a deep drag and holds it before exhaling. "Yes, he's real. He comes down here now and again. Drops off sandwiches and bottles of water."

Wow. That, I wasn't expecting. "Why are you scared of him, then?"

Mary shakes her head and takes another drag. "Have you seen the papers? The man's a monster. He doesn't just kill, he tortures. I wouldn't want to be the one that captures his attention."

My brows furrow. "But—"

"Child, not all monsters are all bad. The Carver is one of 'em. If rumors are true, he enjoys the killing. But he also seems to give a shit about those of us with nothing." She drops the butt on the ground and puts it out with her boot. "He doesn't like people talkin' about him and has ears everywhere. I don't wanna know why you're interested in him, but I'd be careful."

"What about where he lives or what he looks like?"

Mary's eyes grow big, and she backs away, shaking her head. "Dolly, you're gonna get yourself killed. I'll have nothin' to do with it. Leave it alone." With one last worried glance my way, she scuttles out of the alley and rejoins the others.

I make my way down the opposite end, coming out onto Dionysus Square. Out of the periphery, I notice a hand reaching for me, and I dodge out of the way. A short man, dressed in ratty clothes, peers at me with watery blue eyes. "The Carver's coming for you," he says with a cackle. He throws his arms out, tilts his head toward the stormy sky, and spins in a slow circle. "The Carver is coming for us all."

A shiver of apprehension slides down my spine, and I hurry away, my feet eager to put distance between us. The entire way back to the warehouse, I feel eyes on me. I know there can't be—it's impossible—but logic doesn't seem to be my friend right now.

Hysteria rides my back until I'm safely in the warehouse with the door bolted behind me. I suck in ragged breaths and try to shake off whatever has my blood in a frenzy. It was just some random man. *Calm down. There's no way you could be on Sinister's radar.*

Once my breathing returns to normal, I stride across the warehouse, pull open the hidden panel, and jog up the stairs to my room. The problem is, I don't have enough information. But there is someone—two someones, actually—who might help.

There are advantages to being friends with hackers' wives.

Throwing myself onto my mattress, I grab my laptop from under my pillow and boot it up. It's seen better days but works well enough for what I need it to. In the top left corner, an icon of a red kiss with blood dripping from it glows with a pulsating light. I click on it, and the screen goes black before the picture clears, showing me a room I haven't seen before. Sunlight pours through the windows of what is clearly a living room, making me frown. It should be dark outside.

"Hello?" I say, wondering if the connection went awry.

The room spins as someone on their end turns the laptop around. My face breaks into a smile when a pretty blonde woman around my age comes into view. She returns my grin with one of her own, her eyes lighting up when she sees me. "Dolly! How are you? It's been a while since we've heard from you." She sets the laptop on a table next to her so I can better see her.

"Is that Dolly?" another voice says, and a woman with curly brown hair and bright-aqua eyes peers into the screen. I give her a little wave, almost embarrassed at the attention.

"Move, bitches, I wanna say hi," a third voice says. The woman it belongs to has brown hair and eyes, and tattoos covering one arm. She leaps over the back of the couch they're sitting on, forcing herself between the other two.

Tessa, Rebecca, and Dutch. Or my guardian angels, as I call them. Two years ago, they stormed into Grammy Lockwood's Home For Girls and obliterated the malicious guards who enjoyed tormenting us. I remember watching with a wide grin on my face as they took them out, one by one. While the other girls cowered in corners, I had crept closer to watch, and when they captured the cruel bitch that made our lives a living hell, I asked to help torture the cunt.

I enjoyed every second of it.

Does that make me as evil as them? I give a mental shrug. But I never hurt the innocent. Perhaps enjoying the bloodshed makes me fucked up. I'm sure the morality police would happily lock me away and throw away the key.

But they won't do the hard work I'm willing to do. What Tessa, Rebecca, and Dutch do every day. Not everyone deserves life, to breathe the same as the rest of us. I fully understand the hypocrisy. I'm not a good person either. Thirteen people have lost their lives because of me. Maybe I don't deserve to live, and perhaps one day, someone will take me out too. And that's okay.

I refuse to feel remorse for taking the lives of pedophiles and abusers. I'll willingly accept a place in hell if it means I can spare even one child from the horrors I faced.

My guardian angels know all about hard lives. Tessa's parents and uncle routinely abused her. Rebecca grew up in a house full of horrors no child should ever endure. Dutch's father was the ultimate monster—a villain so evil, he gave the devil himself a run for his money.

The justice system failed us all, as it routinely does for so many. They may call us murderers and vigilantes, but we do what the system refuses to—take out the trash. The world is a better place without them in it, and I won't apologize for it.

The four of us make a little small talk before I get down to why I contacted them. "I was wondering if Eric or Trey might do a little research for me," I ask. Eric is one of Tessa's husbands—she has two—and Trey is Rebecca's. Both are hackers and are scarily good at what they do.

A head of black curls lowers over the top of the screen, and two gray eyes blink at me upside down. A startled laugh pulls from me as I tilt my head to the side. "Hi, Eric."

The screen spins again, making me dizzy, and Eric's full

face appears—the right way up this time. "Why would you even bother asking Trey when I'm the best?" he teases.

"Fuck off, you little asshole," a deep voice shouts.

Eric carries us into the kitchen and plops the laptop on the counter. Trey, an older Black man with short hair and a trimmed beard, comes into view. He raises a coffee cup in my direction in lieu of a hello.

He doesn't talk much, unless it's to Rebecca.

"What can we do for you?" Eric asks.

"There's this man—"

Eric places his chin on his palm and waggles his brows. "A man, huh? Go on, tell me more." A large hand appears out of nowhere and slaps the back of his head. "Ow. Don't be jealous, Nate. You know I love you."

I suck my lips into my mouth to keep from laughing. Nate is Eric's husband and Tessa's other husband. They've got a ménage thing going on. They bicker for a moment, and a familiar pang hits my chest. I rub it absently, feeling tendrils of jealousy rising.

They all had horrific childhoods like mine. Tessa and Rebecca suffered from repeated sexual abuse. They understand what it's like to cower in fear and have a deep familiarity with terror. Yet the three of them have successful relationships. All three are married to men who adore them, who would kill for them or lay down their lives for them in a heartbeat. They've found happiness and love in a world filled with cruelty.

What would that be like? To find your perfect match, one who would burn the world for you? A lump forms in my throat as Nate ruffles Eric's hair before moving away from the screen. Could I ever trust a man enough to give myself to them?

I force the sheen of tears to dissipate and clear my throat. Eric drops the goofy smile and straightens his shoulders. The one thing I love about all of them is that they have never looked at me with pity—even when they found me in the home, dressed in rags and covered in lice.

"So, this man," Eric says. "Tell us about him." He and Trey listen as I repeat the little I know about Sinister. While Eric's face remains impassive, the more I go on, the more Trey scowls.

"He sounds dangerous," Trey says after I've finished. "Why involve yourself in his affairs?"

"I just—" I sigh and run a hand through my hair. "I came back here after you guys rescued me because I need justice. Not just for me, but for my family too. For all the children caught up in their corrupted system. I have to do something; I can't just stand back and let it continue."

"But this Sinister guy sounds a bit like us," Eric replies. "If the rumors are true about him, that is. It's possible he's simply a hitman for that O'Brien guy you mentioned, but it sounds like he might be on his own mission."

"That's what I want to find out. If he's a serial killer with a torture kink—"

"I resent that implication!" Tessa calls out from the living room, making me chuckle.

"I need to know," I continue. "On the other hand, if he's like me, it would be nice to know I have a possible ally if I needed one. Not sure how I'd make his acquaintance, but stranger things have happened. Like getting rescued by you guys."

Eric sits back and folds his arms over his chest. "Alright. Trey and I will look into him. If he's as secretive as you suggest, it might take us a couple of days."

I offer him a smile. "Thank you both. I appreciate it." Glancing again at the bright windows in the background, I ask, "Where are you, anyway?" They're based in New York City, so it should be as dark there as it is here.

"Australia. We're hunting down a large trafficking ring."

31

"Don't fuck with the kangaroos. I hear they have a nasty kick."

Eric chuckles. "Cruz already had an encounter with one. Kangaroo: one, Cruz: zero." I laugh, picturing Dutch's husband fighting the marsupial. After we say our goodbyes, I shut down the encrypted connection and lean back against the scratched metal wall posing as a headboard.

Why did that body have to turn up so close to my warehouse? I've managed to ignore the whispers I've heard about The Carver for two whole years. Now, he's all I can think about, especially after Eric's comment about him "being like us."

My stomach rumbles, reminding me I have eaten nothing since the small basket of fries at the bar. I slide off the mattress and check I have some money left in my pocket. I'll get something to eat and maybe scout out the docklands. Perhaps I'll find some information on Sinister on my own while I wait for Eric or Trey to get back to me.

CHAPTER FIVE

SINISTER

I stride through Aidan O'Brien's compound, sweeping my gaze over the marble floors and along the art-covered walls. People scramble out of my way when they notice the heavy scowl on my face, the terror in their eyes doing little to placate my inner monster. It's the anniversary of Wren's death, and every year, I go into the woods to remember her and search for her remains. She deserves a proper burial, even though I know the possibility of finding any trace of her after all this time is unlikely.

Having it interrupted by an urgent message from the IT department has turned my already sour mood into a homicidal one.

After pulling me out of the Aries River, Aidan took me home with him. Once I'd recovered from the beating and near drowning, he put me to work. At the time, I would have gnawed my own arm off for the man. Not only did he rescue me, but he gave me a home, food, affection, and a purpose. It was the first time since my parents' deaths that someone other than Wren was kind to me, and I held on to it with every fiber of my being.

I would—and did—anything he asked of me.

As the years passed, he treated me like his own son. I received the finest education, learned martial arts, and how to use a variety of weapons. The regular exercise and three meals a day transformed the skinny teenager into a highly disciplined and honed man.

When I was sixteen, I executed my first kill. I no longer remember his name, but he had been one of Aidan's men. He thought he could steal from the Irishman and no one would notice. Aidan wanted me to make an example of him, and so I did.

That day, The Carver was born.

On my eighteenth birthday, Aidan declared me his heir. Dissenters were quickly dispatched, and the blood-soaked floors of the compound served as a warning to anyone else who had an issue with it.

Guilt would plague most individuals when it comes to taking a life, but consciences are funny things. My time with Richard changed me on a fundamental level. Sinclair is well and truly gone and has been since he went into the river. When I take a life, I feel nothing even closely resembling remorse. Every man I kill deserves to die.

That was the one stipulation I made the first time Aidan ordered me to kill. Only the guilty, and under no circumstances would I hurt a child. He's never asked me to do otherwise, and I've never broken that vow.

I throw the basement door open and jog down the stairs, my boots echoing on the metal treads. The members of the geek squad don't bother looking up from their computers as I storm past. They're like moles, rarely peeking their heads out of the underground, as evidenced by their red-rimmed eyes and pale skin.

If they ever remade Bram Stoker's *Dracula*, they would nail the part through their looks alone.

Turning right, I duck into the service room, following the maze-like paths through walls of computers. Neon purple-

and-blue lights flash and blink, looking like something out of a science fiction movie.

The door of the little office hiding at the back of the room might be closed, but I don't bother knocking, and stride in like I own the place. Carlos, the head IT guy, flicks his gaze up at me before going back to work.

"You should learn to knock," he mutters as his fingers fly over the keyboard.

"You should learn respect," I counter.

Carlos lets loose a long-suffering sigh. He stretches his arms into the air, leans back in his chair, and gives me a once-over. "Could you look any more like a thug?" he asks, gesturing at me.

I glance down, my brow furrowing. Steel-capped boots, black jeans, black T-shirt, black sweater. All that's missing is my overcoat, but Aidan prefers to keep the compound's temperature at a sauna-like level, so I don't wear it inside.

"What's wrong with it?" I ask.

"Nothing. Forget I said anything."

I scoff and throw myself into the highly uncomfortable chair facing his desk. "I doubt you texted me to chat about my wardrobe. What's so urgent?"

"You know the saying, 'don't kill the messenger'?"

"Yes."

"So don't, okay? I'm not ready to end up in the bay yet. Still have shit to do." My fists clench, making Carlos gulp. There are very few people I tolerate. Carlos is one of them, but I'm really not in the mood for bullshit today. "Okay, okay. Keep your shirt on, Sin."

"Don't call me that," I say, anger threading my words. It's what Wren used to call me—I won't allow anyone else to.

Carlos glides his chair back, putting distance between us. "Sorry, Sinister. My apologies. I see it's one of those days."

A low growl rumbles in my chest, and his face pales. *Fuck.* "I apologize. It's a bad day, Carlos. Just get on with it, okay?"

He eyes me warily but gives a nod. "You asked me to inform you if I noticed anyone searching for you online."

"And?" It's a regular occurrence. Some of Arcadia's citizens want me dead. Others, like the girls on Eros Lane, see me as some kind of dark superhero. And the rest are just downright terrified. I would expect searches. But Carlos wouldn't call me here for everyday, run-of-the-mill searches.

"Yesterday, there was a new flurry of searches on you coming from outside of Arcadia. That wouldn't generally be concerning. After all, people talk, and the city isn't a prison. Might've been someone curious after hearing stories. But this? This is something different."

I sit straighter. "Different how?"

"They're coming in on two fronts. Social media, news outlets, police files...they're hitting everything, leaving no stone unturned. I don't know who they are, but their encryption is next-level. And before you ask, no, I can't track them."

"What else?"

"They're attempting to hack our servers."

My fingers tap my knee. "Will they get in?"

When Carlos's face loses all sense of humor, I know it's serious. In all the years I've known him, I'm not sure I've ever seen him look so blank. "Yes."

"Yes?" I jump to my feet and lean my hands on his desk. "What do you mean, yes?"

"They're good. Like, really good. You know I'm excellent at what I do, Sinister. It's why Aidan hired me. I'm one of the best. But this?" He waves his hand toward the large window overlooking the server room. "This is beyond anything I can deal with."

"Shut it down."

"If I do—"

"Can we recover?" I demand.

Carlos hesitates but nods. "There might be losses, though.

I can't accurately predict the outcome. But Sinister, Aidan—"
I slice my hand through the air.

"I'll deal with him. The important thing is keeping the business and Aidan's assets safe." I move toward the door before turning back. "Out of curiosity, were there any searches on Aidan? Or just me?"

"Just you."

I hum and leave his office. As I walk back through the maze, the computer lights go dark, and the fans slow before cutting off. An eerie silence falls over the room, and the staff drift from their desks to stand at the doorways to their offices, watching me as I stride past them.

Who the fuck is searching for me? And why?

"Do what you need to do," Aidan says weakly before racking coughs render him speechless. My chest aches at the sight of the man I've come to see as a father figure. He'll only be seventy on his next birthday, and if it wasn't for the cancer spreading throughout his body, I would have expected him to see many more years.

The one bonus of him having established me as his heir ten years ago—and having the reputation I do—means the transition of power should go smoothly after his passing. However, I can't ensure there won't be another attempted coup, whether from internal or external forces, so I have resorted to bribery and threats to maintain secrecy regarding his medical condition.

Someday, I'll weed out all the corruption plaguing Arcadia and return it to what it once was. But until then, I'll do what I need to do.

I snatch the cup of ice water off the trolley sitting by his bed and cradle his head so he can sip from the straw. The nurse sitting in the corner watches me with wide eyes, but I ignore her. She has nothing to fear from me as long as she does her job and takes care of Aidan the way he deserves.

After straightening his blanket, I leave the depressing room and tamp down on my feelings. With the anniversary, the unknown hacking threat, and Aidan's looming death, not keeping my emotions in check could be disastrous.

It's too bad I've been unable to locate the other men responsible for Wren's death. Spilling blood would go a long way toward soothing my mood. My hands curl into fists, and the corner of my mouth lifts. That's precisely what I need.

Let's go hunting.

CHAPTER SIX

SINISTER

The full moon peeks from behind silvery clouds, blazing a white trail over the gently lapping waves of Hera Bay. A salty breeze pats my shoulders and ruffles my hair before moving on, leaving me alone with my thoughts.

My hands tighten around the rusted railing that blocks the unwary from falling into the bay. Passivity is not my strong suit, and it's becoming more difficult to ignore the eyes on me.

It started three days after Carlos shut the computers down two weeks ago. They've followed me downtown, into the hills, and along the Aries. They watched when I savagely beat a man for attacking a woman and when I handed out food bags to the women working Eros Lane.

The only time the feeling disappears is when I'm at the compound. Now, I'm not a paranoid man, but I pay attention to my instincts. They rarely steer me wrong. Still, I might have doubted myself if I hadn't caught my stalker's reflection in passing store windows or car side mirrors.

They dress in all black, with a hoodie pulled low to hide their face. I'm unsure whether it's a teen boy or a woman, but

I'm leaning more toward a woman. It's in the way they move, the way their arms swing when they walk.

I've led them on a merry dance around the city, cataloging clues they unwittingly let slip. I also wanted to check their dedication. How long would they follow me? After two weeks, I can safely say they don't have commitment issues.

Spinning around, I sweep my gaze over the surrounding warehouses, and the corner of my mouth lifts when my stalker ducks back into the shadows. I'm done with the cat-and-mouse game. It's time to turn the hunted into the hunter.

They take off into an alley, and my feet pick up their pace as I hurry after them. I'll give my stalker credit for bravery; they never once turn their head. They know there's a monster at their back, but they keep to the shadows and continue trying to dodge me.

It almost works. My gaze catches on the fire escape above me. I come to a stop, letting my stalker out of my sight before leaping up and grabbing the rungs of the ladder. A grunt punches out of me as I pull my bodyweight up and land awkwardly on the metal grating. After taking a moment to catch my breath, I race up to the roof, hoping they're still within view. I stride along the edge, searching the alley. *There.* My stalker crouches behind a dumpster, peering out around the side. I lean my elbows on the short concrete balustrade, watching with interest as they wait a full ten minutes before creeping out and disappearing around the corner.

I follow along, noticing they never look up. They remove a key from their pocket and push into a warehouse, closing the door behind them with a last glance over their shoulder. *Gotcha, little stalker.*

Now that my stalker knows I'm on to them, I find myself curious what course of action they'll take next.

≈

IT DOESN'T ESCAPE my notice that the stalking began after the flurry of online searches. After I chased them four days ago, the feeling of being watched disappeared, and I can only assume I scared them off. Or they've changed tactics, and I just haven't caught on yet. I almost miss the steady presence following me, which makes my brows furrow in consternation. Why the fuck would I miss it? Perhaps because their presence never felt malicious but more curious.

It was like they were learning me, or maybe trying to understand me. It's a foreign concept for me after becoming used to the terror I usually receive from the population. It felt...nice.

No. I can't have that. Niceness has no place in my life. Torture, fear, blood, revenge, control. Those are what keep me going, what make my blood sing.

So why does my little stalker intrigue me so? Why do my thoughts turn toward them over and over again, especially now they've stopped shadowing me?

I've stayed away from the docklands, but I find myself drawn toward it. Curiosity makes me want to discover who they are, what they want, what motivates them. It's not like I can't dispatch them if they pose a threat to me or Aidan.

Mind made up, I lope up the stairs to my private apartment in Aidan's compound. It's not much but has a small bedroom, living room, kitchenette, and bathroom. I'm grateful for the privacy it offers, as not everyone that lives here gets their own room, let alone a whole apartment.

After a quick shower, I dress in all-black tactical gear, including a ski mask and leather gloves. Knives disappear into various pockets, and I strap my pistol into a holster at my side. Once I'm ready, I make my way to the garage and pick out one of Aidan's many cars. Tonight is not the time to stand out, so I choose the Maybach over the sports cars.

I avoid dwelling on the fact that the silently waiting supercars will soon belong to me. My fingers tighten around the steering wheel at the thought of losing another parental figure. I'd happily give up the cars and money if it meant Aidan living another twenty years.

He isn't perfect. His hands are as bloody as mine. But he took in a lonely, scared, starving kid and nursed him back to health. Not only that, but gave him the means to enact his revenge, through both education and practice. And for that, I'll be forever in his debt.

The fifteen-minute drive flies past while I'm deep in thought. I park the car two blocks from my stalker's warehouse and double-check my weapons before making my way over to it. It's a good thing Aidan collects information and hordes it like Richard did food. Since I couldn't use the computers, I found satellite images of Arcadia that Aidan keeps in his personal library, along with the blueprints for that building.

What are the odds they chose a warehouse once belonging to Aidan's rival? If they knew he owned it now, I doubt they would have chosen that one. Whether they picked it purposefully or it was a coincidence, I'm grateful for it, as it allowed me to memorize its layout.

It may not have any windows for me to spy through, but the roof has a large skylight that covers around a third of it. And even better, it has three access points—one accessed through a stairwell, and two others through hatches above a narrow industrial catwalk that surrounds three sides of the interior.

My dear friend adrenaline comes along for the ride as I once again climb the metal fire escape to the roof, making my blood sing. I walk around the perimeter, mapping it out in my mind by the orange glow of the streetlights. The strong breeze tugs at my clothes, bringing with it the scent of rotting fish. My nostrils twitch, but I ignore it while I investigate.

They locked the door with chains and heavy locks, leaving me with no choice but to use one of the hatches. Hopefully, they don't know about them and haven't sealed them up or blocked access to them.

My luck holds. The one on the right side hides beneath a layer of gravel the designers used to cover the roof to protect it from UV rays and hail. When a soft glow lights up the skylight, I peer down into it, my brows lowering when I realize they've divided the warehouse into sections.

This is interesting. Smugglers once used the warehouse to store illegal goods and installed pull-out walls to hide merchandise from inspectors—back when Arcadia still had some of her conscience left. Metal tracks run along the floor, and the walls can be positioned in a multitude of configurations.

My little stalker has positioned them so they divide the building into three. Well, to be more precise—seven. A small foyer-type area near the front door, followed by a larger area split into four rooms, and another smaller area in the back, housing the overseer's office and bathrooms.

The four-room split resembles a home with a kitchen, bedroom, living room, and bathroom. Since there's no plumbing, the kitchen and bathroom aren't usable—so this is for show. But why? My head cants to the left, and I realize what's nagging at me.

Without ceilings, it resembles a dollhouse.

Curiosity piqued, I head over to the hatch, swipe away the gravel, and pry it open. I gently lower myself down onto the metal catwalk so as not to alert them of my presence. I can get a better view of the layout from here, safe in the knowledge that I'm hidden in the shadows.

Just as I settle down and cross my legs, a young woman appears from behind the far back wall panel. She wears a flowy light-blue dress decorated with pink flowers, knee-high socks, and girlish shoes. Why is she dressed like a child? Unease pierces my chest as she closes the panel and skips through the dollhouse to the foyer.

The lights dim as three loud knocks boom through the building. She runs a hand down her dress, straightens her shoulders, and pulls the door open. If she speaks, I'm unable to hear it, but she appears to welcome a man inside. She takes his coat before leading him to the living room, and my fists clench when he grabs her ass.

She spins around and shakes her finger at him while her other hand covers her mouth in pretend shock. It's...like a play. She dances around him while he watches her with his hand covering his dick. What the fuck?

I pull out a pair of opera glasses from one of my pockets. They may be an odd choice, but they're less conspicuous than binoculars. My breath catches in my throat when I zero in on the man—Evan Hopper, one of the men that took Wren. My fingers tighten around the glasses, and I have to hold back the tide of anger threatening to take over.

A loud crash rings out, focusing my attention. The woman dashes away from the couch and disappears. The lights briefly go out before blue ones switch on, revealing painted words etched on the walls. I freeze as each one seems to punch me in the gut.

Murderer. Rapist. Abuser. Pedo. Liar. Thief. Adulterer. Bigot. Racist.

An eerily beautiful voice rises to the rafters, the words sending a shiver down my spine. Evan pulls himself off the couch, clutching his head as he hobbles away. Instead of heading toward the door, he stumbles into the bathroom and trips over the toilet.

"Ring around the rosie..." The woman seems to melt out of the wall, and it's then I notice just how thick they are. There must be passageways inside them. Clever girl. *"A pocket full of posies..."* Evan scrambles to his feet and veers into the kitchen. My little stalker enters from the opposite side, swinging a bat.

"No, please!" Evan shouts, raising his hands and backing away.

"Ashes, ashes..." Evan turns on his heel, but it's too late. The bat swings in a vicious arc and connects with the back of his knees. *"We all fall down."*

My dick hardens so fast, my head spins with the loss of blood. Jesus fucking Christ. She's magnificent. Who the hell is she?

The woman uses her foot to press against his shoulder, flipping him over. Tears stream down the man's face as he begs for mercy. She withdraws something from her pocket and shoves it in front of his face.

"I'm sorry! I'm sorry!" he cries, raising his hands to cover his head.

"We all fall down," she repeats, lifting the bat above her head. She swings it repeatedly until blood splatters the walls and cabinets and he's no longer moving. As I lean forward, the catwalk emits a rusty squeak. She spins around, her eyes narrowing as she scans the warehouse. I hold my breath, not daring to move in case she somehow spots me. But true to form, she doesn't glance up, and after a moment, turns away and begins to clean up the mess she made.

SHE SLEEPS WITH A NIGHT-LIGHT.

I waited for an hour after she retired before searching her out. She turned the overseer's office into a bedroom, if you can call it that. A thin mattress more suitable for a prison lies on the floor, complete with one blanket and two thin pillows. The rest of the room contains little else—a dressing table, a mirror, and a small railing with a few items of clothing. Her famous hoodie lies abandoned on a stool with mended legs.

After pocketing my gloves, I drop to my haunches and study my little stalker better. She lies on her side in the fetal position with her fist tucked under her chin. The pale glow from the night-light gives off just enough light to illuminate the soft skin of her cheeks and the fan of dark lashes hiding her eyes from me.

Who is she? The intricate warehouse setup, combined with her obvious skill, suggests this isn't her first time killing, and most likely won't be her last.

It's rare that someone intrigues me. I care about Aidan and my revenge and very little else. I suppose, if I'm honest, I also have my minuscule list of "tolerables" that I wouldn't want harm to come to. But you won't find me asking about their families, or if they even have any. We don't go for beers or watch the game together.

I just don't care.

So this morbid fascination for this girl, who doesn't look older than twenty or so, is curious. My arm reaches out, unbidden, and I ghost my thumb over her cheek.

Only to find myself flat on my back a moment later with a knife to my throat.

CHAPTER SEVEN
DOLLY

My lips curl into a smile as I stare down at my prey. "'Will you walk into my parlor? said the Spider to the Fly.'" I tilt my head and reach out to tear his ski mask off. Years of controlling my features save me from gasping. He's beautiful. Even lying on the ground, I can tell he's tall and well built. His dark-brown hair begs my fingers to run through the silky-looking strands, while thick lashes line eyes that match the color of his hair. Light stubble edges a firm jaw, and his full lips make me want to test their softness.

The grainy pictures Eric found before they shut down the compound's computers didn't do The Carver justice. Not one bit.

"I suppose I'm the fly in this scenario?" Sinister asks in a husky voice. He lifts his head, but I smack my hand against his forehead and push it back down. Little sparks dance across my skin, and I wipe it against my thigh as my brow creases. What was that?

"It took you long enough," I murmur, pressing the knife closer to his Adam's apple. "I was expecting you at least a week ago."

His eyebrows climb to his hairline. "Mmm. Well played,

little stalker. You've trapped your fly in your web. What will you do now?"

"I suppose that dep—" I shriek as he knocks my knife away and spins us around so he's on top. He presses himself into the cradle of my thighs, his hard length brushing against me. My mouth dries as I blink up at him, unused to the feeling of heat pooling in my core.

After the systemic abuse I suffered most of my life, I never dreamed I'd be in a position where I'd find myself wondering what a man tasted like. I've never had consensual sex, and besides my occasional yearnings for companionship—generally after seeing my guardian angels with their men—I never thought it was something I'd even want.

But I do now. How would it be to kiss someone for the first time? To actually invite someone's touch, to give myself to someone because I wanted to, not because I'm forced?

"If you keep looking at me like that, we're going to have a very different kind of conversation. One that starts with me peeling that silky nightie off you and ending with you coming all over my cock." His words spike a fever inside me, and my heart speeds up. Sinister groans and presses his forehead against mine. "Fuck. I can smell your desire, little stalker."

We stare into each other's eyes as our breaths mingle. Something hot and electric passes between us, and my hips lift of their own volition, grinding against him.

"Dolly," I whisper before turning my head away. I can't keep staring into his eyes. It's as if he's drawing me toward an abyss, one I might not come out of the same if I were to let go and jump into it.

"Dolly?" Sinister repeats, pressing his palms against the floor and lifting himself off me just enough to see me clearly. I immediately miss his heat and the way his body feels against mine.

What? No, I don't. Distance is good. Yep. Good.

"My name."

Sinister brushes a knuckle over my cheek, the small contact breaking something inside me. I can't do this. I can't let anyone see the disaster I am inside. Shoving his hand, I squirm out from under him and scramble away. I can only imagine what I look like to him: small, trembling, pressed against the wall like a cornered animal.

But that's what I am now, what they made me.

Sinister growls and leaps to his feet in a fluid movement that shouldn't be hot but is. He grabs my arm, pulls me to my feet, and cuffs my neck with his hand. I whimper, and he freezes before a sly grin spreads across his face.

"Oh, Dolly, I think you're going to be the ruin of me," he whispers before brushing his lips against mine in a breath of a kiss. My tongue darts out to wet my lips, and he groans again, pushing his face against my neck and breathing harshly. A part of me wants him to slam inside me and show me what sex should be.

Another part of me wants to run screaming into the night, putting as much distance between us as possible. The thought of him chasing after me makes my knees buckle.

"Fuck it," he mutters. His powerful arms close around me and haul me against him. His lips crash against mine, and my entire body lights up like the Fourth of July. I tangle my fingers in his hair, tugging on the strands as his tongue forces its way into my mouth.

I can't breathe. I can't think. Sinister invades every one of my senses, dominating my body in a way that leaves me dizzy and wanting more. My legs wrap around his waist, and my pussy clenches, desperate to be filled by him. He slams me against the wall and rips my nightie over my head, leaving me wearing nothing but thin cotton panties.

"You're so fucking beautiful," he says against the column of my neck, pressing fervent kisses downward until he sucks a nipple into his mouth. My back arches as I cry out, pressing his head tighter to me. He sucks as much of my tit into his mouth as possible, using his teeth to scrape along my delicate flesh.

Each touch burns like I'm on fire, and I finally understand what all the songs were talking about. Sinister pulls me away from the wall and settles me on the mattress, his large hands that wield knives and take lives surprisingly gentle as they pull my panties down my legs.

"Open for me, little stalker," he says, and I obey. Lust blazes in his eyes, but it doesn't scare me, not like it used to at Grammy Lockwood's. He touches me like I'm worth caring about, making tears spring to my eyes.

He freezes and sits back on his knees. "Tell me to stop, and I will." I suck my bottom lip into my mouth and nod. He doesn't realize the meaning of my tears, and now isn't the time to tell him.

If I ever tell him.

How do you tell a man that you were raped repeatedly by numerous men? That you stopped fighting after the first year because you learned it didn't matter. No amount of screaming stopped them, and it only earned me beatings or extended stays in solitary—a minuscule closet Grammy would lock me in for days at a time.

I shove the thoughts away into a little box and lock it up tight when Sinister strips out of his clothes. He has broad shoulders and chest, a narrow waist, and a delicious V that points to his thick cock. A tattoo of a bird rests over his heart, but the rest of his skin is unadorned.

A little voice in my head pipes up, asking if I'm really about to sleep with someone I just met. I tell it to shut up. I've never had anything solely for myself, and even if this lasts only one night, it's something I can hold close when loneliness sets in.

Sinister kneels on the mattress and spreads my legs wider. I drop my head back and let my eyes fall closed, my hands twisting into the blanket. And then nearly jump out of my skin at the first touch of his warm tongue along my slit. He chuckles and places a large hand on my stomach, holding me down.

No one could accuse Sinister of not knowing what he's doing. The man zeros in on my clit like it contains a homing device, making my breath catch in my throat and my arousal leak down my legs. He hums his approval, lapping it up like it's the finest wine. His hand presses tighter on my stomach when I writhe beneath him, trying to escape his hold.

"Please, Sinister," I beg as the pleasure tightens in my core. He chuckles and slides a finger inside me. My walls clamp down on it, and I let out a moan of frustration. It's not enough. I need more.

"Tell me what you need, little stalker," he says, his gaze jumping from my face to my breasts, then down to where his finger joins me.

"More. Fuck. Please!" He presses a second finger in and curls them. I shriek, my back coming off the bed at the powerful sensation.

"So fucking responsive," Sinister says, working his fingers over the sensitive bundle of nerves while this thumb rubs my clit. "Scream my name when you come, Dolly. I want all of Arcadia to know you're mine."

I'm mine. I should protest his audacity at claiming me like a caveman, but the thought vanishes when my orgasm tears through me with a force that leaves me blind and gasping. I soar out into space and scream his name to the universe, my body fully onboard with the idea of belonging to this dangerous man, even if my mind isn't.

Yet.

"Yes, that's it. Such a good girl." Sinister pulls my legs farther apart and slams deep inside me. My mouth opens on a silent scream before he crushes his mouth to mine. All I can taste is him. All I can think of is him. All I can smell is him.

My legs wrap around his waist, pulling him closer as he

pounds into me. He murmurs nonsense in my ear, telling me things like *you're such a good girl* and *you're so fucking wet for me, baby.*

"I'm going to come so deep inside you, little stalker. Going to fill you up with my cum until it spills out of this pretty pussy and leaks down your legs," Sinister says. Drops of sweat fall from his face to mine, mingling together.

"Please," I whine, his dirty talk making me wetter. The room fills with the sounds of our harsh breaths and bodies coming together in a frantic race to cross the finish line. My nerves sing as the pleasure ramps up a second time, and a grin tears across Sinister's face, giving him a savage look.

"Yes, come for me, Dolly. I need you to shatter around my cock when I release inside you." He shoves his hand between us and pinches my clit, while biting down on my nipple at the same time. My back bows when my orgasm claims me, and Sinister follows a moment later. He stays inside me, rocking in and out, staring down at where our bodies join. When he meets my eyes, my mouth dries at the possessive look in them. "You shouldn't have allowed me to do that, little stalker. Now that I've had you, I'm never letting you go."

MY FINGERTIPS TRACE over his tattoo as I cuddle into Sinister's side. I'm...happy, I think. Content, at the very least. They aren't emotions I'm overly familiar with, but I'm not going to dwell on them overmuch.

My body is sated, my mind is still a little numb from the orgasms, and I'm too lazy to do anything but bask in the feeling of safety being in his arms brings.

I shouldn't feel like this, not so quickly. But there's something about Sinister that makes me trust him—and not because he knows how to wring pleasure from me when I never fathomed it was possible. It's an innate feeling, something residing so deep inside me I can't identify it. But it's there, all the same.

"Tell me the story about this," I murmur, tapping on his tattoo. He shifts beneath my head, his pecs flexing as he turns to place a chaste kiss on my sweat-dampened forehead.

"It's for my sister," he replies, his hand coming up to take mine in his. He tangles our fingers together before going silent again.

"Sister?" I ask, wanting to keep him talking. I want to learn more about him.

"Foster sister, to be more precise. She was killed fourteen years ago, and I got the tattoo to remind me of her. She's the reason I became The Carver. I wanted to get revenge on the men that hurt her."

A lump forms in my throat, and I tighten my fingers around his. "I'm so sorry, Sinister. Why a bird, though?"

"It's a wren. Her name was—"

My veins fill with ice water, and I yank myself away from him. Backing away from the bed, I stumble over my feet as I shake my head. "No." Sinister jumps up and advances toward me, his face wreathed in confusion. I put my hands up and retreat until my back crashes into the wall. "It's impossible. You—you're dead."

Why does my chest hurt? I glance down at it, and my body staggers as black spots dance around my vision. My hands cover my heart as images from the past slam into my mind. I raise my head and reach my arm toward my dead brother—the boy whose body I watched Richard throw into the river.

"Sin?"

CHAPTER EIGHT
SINISTER

" S in?"

Agonizing pain tears through my chest, and I freeze in place as my mind scrambles to keep up. Dolly —no, Wren—sways and her eyes roll up into the back of her head. I leap forward and grab her before she can crumble to the floor.

I crush her body to mine, still reeling. It can't be. She can't be Wren. Richard said he killed her, and Jack confirmed it—he even taunted me about it. This has to be a joke. I plop back down on the mattress, cradling my sister in my arms. As much as my mind balks at the idea, my heart whispers the truth.

My thumb runs over her forehead, searching for the little dent she got when Richard knocked her against the corner of a wall. It's there, and fourteen years of grief and guilt spill out of me. Tears stream down my face as I rock her in my arms. I tell her over and over again how sorry I am. How no one will hurt her again. That she'll never be alone.

While the words pour from my mouth, my conscience screams, *You just fucked your sister.* But she isn't my sister, is she? Not really. We're not blood related, and we didn't grow up together. *Stop trying to come up with rationalizations. You. Just. Fucked. Her.*

After all these years, *now* my conscience wants to make an appearance? It can fuck right off. We did nothing wrong. The woman I watched kill a man, isn't the innocent little eight-year-old she once was. I don't know where she's been all this time or what's happened to her since I last saw her, but I know one thing for sure.

She's like me.

I changed the day Richard threw me off the bridge. I was no longer Sinclair, but Sinister. And I have the feeling Wren is the same. Why else would she call herself Dolly, if not to reinvent herself? We aren't the same downtrodden children who spent three years together in Limp Dick's fortress. We're something different. Tougher, stronger, more jaded.

Killers.

Our executions may differ in style, but we're doing the same thing, aren't we? Taking out the trash. Pride blooms in my chest when I relive her kill. She took out one of her abductors by herself. My arms tighten around her. *Two down, little bird. Four to go.*

Wren moans and thrashes in my arms. "Sinclair, help!" she cries, her eyes scrunched tight. "No, no. Don't throw him in the river. Let me go!" I keep murmuring my assurances to her, and she eventually quietens, her breathing evening out.

She saw Richard do that? Jesus. Why? Why were they all so invested in making us believe the other was dead? Was it just for the grief it would cause us? Or something else? We may never have all the answers we want, and I'll have to come to terms with that.

I lie back and draw the blanket over us, my mind too busy to fall asleep. When Wren wakes up, we're going to have an honest and open conversation—about everything. I need to know what happened that day, and what her life has been like since. Then, I'm going to take her to meet Aidan. I want her to know the man who saved me and helped me become the man I am today.

After that, we've got plans to make. We're going to take down the other three men, then go after Richard. I've allowed him to walk this earth for far too long—it's time to put him down.

∽

SOFT FOOTSTEPS PLOD down the stairs, and I glance up from the kitchen table. I popped out to a local twenty-four-hour diner and grabbed breakfast while Wren slept. Not only is the kitchen not functional, but the appliances don't work either, and there wasn't a scrap of food to be found anywhere in the warehouse.

Wren's steps slow, and she appears at the entrance. She's donned thin sweats and a T-shirt that have seen better days, and left her hair a tangled mess. Sunlight pours in from the skylight, emphasizing her big blue eyes. If I had seen her up close and in better lighting earlier, I would have known who she was by them alone.

I push the chair back and walk over to her. She stares at me as if I'm a ghost, and I suppose I am. We both thought the other was dead, so being here together feels surreal. A single tear slides down her cheek, and I pull her into my arms. "Shh, little bird. It's going to be all right." Her fingers curl in my shirt, holding on to me like I might disappear again.

After a few minutes, she pushes away, her cheeks blooming rose. She refuses to meet my eye but gestures toward the table. "What's all this?" Her husky voice stirs my cock, remembering how she screamed my name when I made her come.

"Breakfast. Come on and eat."

She sits on the edge of the seat, her fingers plucking at the edge of her shirt. I fill her plate with eggs, bacon, pancakes, and toast, and set it in front of her, along with a tall glass of orange juice. She hesitates, then picks up a fork and begins to eat, hiding her face behind a waterfall of hair.

I let her eat in peace and remain silent while I shovel eggs into my mouth. Her gestures portray her nervousness, and it hits me that I don't know what's going on inside that head of hers. Is she scared? Embarrassed? Or does she regret what we did?

My fist tightens around my fork. She better not. I meant what I told her last night—I won't let her go. So if she's having doubts, she better get over them real quick. The thought of bending her over the table and spanking her until she begs me to fuck her makes my cock harden.

When her plate is half empty, she pushes it away and folds her hands on her lap. "They made me watch," she whispers, her head still lowered. "They held me across the river where you wouldn't see me. One of them covered my mouth so I couldn't scream. And—" Her knuckles turn white as she exhales. "And then Richard threw you in the Aries. He laughed. Even above the sound of the rushing water, I heard him laugh when your body sank beneath the surface."

My appetite dies, and I sit back in my chair as she continues her story in a broken voice. She tells me how after Richard drove away, the men forced her to her knees and made her give them oral. It was their payment for allowing her to witness her brother's death.

"'Now you have no one,' they told me. 'No one will save you, no one will look for you.'" Wren raises her head and pierces me with a haunted look. "I believed them, Sin. I watched you die. And then...then they sold me to Grammy Lockwood."

She tells me about her years at the girls' home located in an adjacent town. It was a front for prostitution and catered to men with particular tastes. "Some of them wanted children.

Others wanted punching bags." She stands and rips her T-shirt off before spinning around to show me her back. I hiss at the old striped scars and cigarette burns. How did I not notice them last night?

I leap to my feet, but Wren shakes her head and backs away. My jaw tics, but I incline my head and sit back down. *It's her story. Shut the fuck up and let her tell it. We can get names out of her later.*

"It didn't take me long to stop fighting. Grammy Lockwood was a thousand times worse than Richard." Her trembling hand comes to the base of her neck, and her eyes fill with tears. "I-I don't want to talk about her. Maybe another day."

I hold my hand out, and my heart lifts when she takes it. She settles on my knee, and I wrap my arm around her waist. "Then, one day, my guardian angels came." She tells me about the three women who busted in and liberated the girls. "They were magnificent. No hesitation, no remorse. They killed all the guards before hunting Grammy through the house. I helped them kill her."

"Who are they? Your angels?"

She cuddles into my neck, and a shiver runs over her shoulders. "They work for a company called the Charon Group. They're...I'm not sure how to describe them. They're who you call if a family member has been kidnapped. Or if you need justice because the system has failed you. But Tessa, Dutch, and Rebecca, along with their husbands, specialize in taking down trafficking rings, abusers, and pedophiles.

"Grammy Lockwood's Home For Girls ended up on their radar, and after they shut it down, they helped the others make new lives. But I didn't want to move somewhere else. I wanted to come back here and get revenge for you, for all the children sold into slavery by the corrupt CPS agents. My guardian angels sparked something in me that day. I want to help others like they do, but I want to do it here." She places a hand on my face and tilts my chin down. "So, I came back to where it all started. Back to where I lost my parents and my home. I came back for you."

I lower my head and brush my lips over hers. She opens for me, and I keep the kiss gentle, languid. She's opened up to me, and I don't want to do anything that will scare her away.

After we break the kiss, I tell her my story. About how I almost gave up when the water closed over my head, because Richard had told me my sister was dead. She twists in my lap and wraps her arms around my neck as I describe meeting Aidan and how he saved me. How I learned and trained and became strong, so that I could avenge her death in the only way I knew how—through blood.

"Why The Carver?" she asks, her breath hot on my neck.

"Aidan saw something dark in me, and he used it to his advantage. He needed someone willing to do what needed to be done, and I was all too happy to volunteer—provided he could prove their guilt. I don't hurt innocent people, Wren. I protect them. Even if that means I spill blood to do so. I won't feel guilty for cleaning up the streets."

"Good," she says, startling me. "We can do it together."

"You'll stay with me? Even though I was once your brother?"

She chuckles. "Do I have an option? I thought you claimed me as yours."

A low growl rumbles in my chest. "Damn fucking straight, you're mine. Try to leave and see what happens. I dare you."

Wren pushes me away, leaps off my lap, and runs out of the kitchen. *Oh, little stalker, you're in trouble now.*

I race after her but spin around when I can't find her. Where did she go?

"One, two, Dolly's coming for you..."

Oh, she wants to play. My cock hardens until it's as stiff as a bat at the sound of her haunting voice. One day, once we've cleaned up Arcadia, I'm going to launch her singing career. She'll be fucking famous.

"Three, four, don't be a bore..."

Who's she calling a bore? I stalk through the bedroom and into the living room, and grunt when a hard object connects with my back, making me collapse to my knees. Two arms wrap around my neck, and Wren huffs a laugh in my ear.

"Too easy, big brother. I'm disappointed."

CHAPTER NINE
WREN

S in chuckles as I leap off his back and dash away. "Oh, no. The big bad Sinister's going to get me." I duck into one of the hidden tunnels, my heart racing with delicious fear at the sound of his steps behind me.

Last night was a revelation. Giving my body to Sin and experiencing what sex should be, changed everything for me. Although the bastards from my past tried their damndest, they didn't break me. I've taken my body back and didn't fall apart at the experience.

Instead, I soared. And they can never take that away from me.

I laugh when Sinister's breath glides against my shoulder, and I pick up my pace. My bare feet skid as I change direction and dash down the tunnel to the left. His arm wraps around my waist, and I shriek, smacking his arm.

He lifts me like I weigh nothing and tosses me over his shoulder. "Put me down!" I cry, but instead of answering, he slaps my ass. "Ouch. What was that for?"

"Being a brat. Now be a good girl and stop talking." My mouth opens in an O when he dumps me over the arm of the couch and rips my sweats down. His zipper undoes and his pants hit the floor.

He swipes a finger through my slit, making me moan. His hand comes down on my ass again, the sharp slap ringing through the warehouse. "I told you to be quiet. Every time you make a noise, I'll spank you."

Indignation sends my head flying up. "Fuck you, Sinister. You—" I yelp as he smacks me again.

He leans over my back and licks my cheek. "Shh, little sister. Your big brother's going to use these pretty holes, and you will not say a fucking word—unless it's screaming my name." He moves off me and runs the head of his cock over my pussy. "Fuck, Wren. That made you wet, didn't it? So fucking dirty. Now take your brother's dick like a good little girl."

My arousal leaks from me, and I shudder as he thrusts into me. I love the way he stretches me, the burn hurting in all the right ways. Sin's right—I am so fucking dirty. My eyes drift close, and I hang on to the couch for dear life as he fucks into me hard enough to move it.

"So fucking good, Wren. I could live inside this pussy," Sinister says with a snarl, his hands tightening around my hips. "I'm going to take this pretty little ass later and fill it up with my cum."

I grab a cushion and bite into it to muffle my cries. It doesn't matter; three more harsh slaps sound out as he punishes me for disobeying him. He works me higher and higher until I scream into the cushion.

"Fuck, yeah, little stalker. Choke my cock. That's it." Sinister increases his tempo and slides his hand under my shirt, grabbing my breasts and squeezing my nipples. "Tell me you like your big brother fucking you."

I learned my lesson—my ass aches with all the slaps, so I say nothing. My molars grind together as another orgasm builds on the back of the first one.

Sin's hand creeps up and cradles my neck. "Say it, Wren."

"I love it when my brother fucks me with his enormous cock," I grind out, pressing my ass back into him. "Now shut up and make me come again."

Sinister grunts and tightens his grip around my neck. It should scare me, but all it does is make me want to beg for him to do it more. I know he won't hurt me, and it's another way for me to feel free.

My orgasm triggers when Sinister stills and pours himself into me. He pulls out of me before yanking me off the couch by my throat and pressing me to him. His other hand winds down my body until he cups me with his palm. "You're mine now, Wren. This pussy is mine. That ass is mine. If you let anyone touch what belongs to me, I'll kill them and fuck you over their dead body. Nod if you understand."

I nod. He might be bad for me, but god, he's oh so right. And being his? Abso-fucking-lutely. Some might call him a monster, but he's my monster, and that's all that matters.

I sit at my dressing table and run a brush through my freshly washed hair. My eyes keep finding Sinister in the mirror, admiring the way his muscles flex as he dresses after our shower.

"I'm assuming your angel friends are responsible for the cyber attack on Aidan's compound?" he asks. He does a little hip jiggle as he pulls his pants up over his ass, making me wet my lips. He turns toward me, and I pretend to be fascinated with my brush. "Wren?"

I spin around and lift a shoulder. "Oops?"

"Thought so," he mutters, running a hand through his hair. "Think you can call it off before Aidan loses any more money? I'd really rather not tell him he's losing hundreds of thousands of dollars because you wanted my attention."

I scoff. "I wasn't trying to get your attention, Carver. I was trying to learn about you."

Sinister swaggers toward me, his face breaking into a grin. I lean back on my stool when he places both hands on the table and stoops over me. "You were curious about me."

My brows kiss my hairline. "So?"

He slides a finger down the side of my face. "Were you thinking about me when you were stalking me all over Arcadia?" His nose brushes mine and he whispers, "Did you come back here and touch yourself after?"

I duck under his arm and skip away. "Wouldn't you like to know." When I reach the doorway, I turn around. "They stopped trying to hack you four days ago and won't try again. Your compound's safe."

SINISTER and I spent the past few days getting to know each other better. He took me out for meals, scowling at anyone that looked at me curiously. We made a trip to the river and found a small embankment where we sat and let the water run over our feet. Sinister drove us to the old fortress in the woods, where we walked hand in hand through the old rooms and relived the better memories of our time there. He took me to meet Aidan, who held our hands and told us to be happy.

We talked, and fucked, and cried, and laughed.

And we came up with a plan. Richard is still nowhere to be found, but the other three men that took me? We know where they are, thanks to some help from Eric and Trey.

"What do you think?" I ask Sin with my hands on my hips. We rearranged The Dollhouse by removing all the furniture and storing it behind the third section. Sinister located more wall panels from God knows where, and we turned the warehouse into a maze. We kept the hidden tunnels and added some fun new additions.

One thing I discovered is how rich Sinister is. I guess being the hitman to the largest Mafia boss in the state has its perks. I've never cared too much about money, beyond being able to buy necessities. Second-hand furniture and clothing suits me fine. But Sin has discovered he's got a thing for providing for me, and I now own more clothes than I ever have in my life and get to have fancy new toys to play with.

I'll never give up Barbie, though. She's my ride or die.

Sinister glances down from the ladder he's on, paint dripping from his brush. He wanted to add more decoration to the walls, so I let him at it. He won't let me turn the blue lights on until he's finished.

"Looks good," he replies, glancing over the warehouse. "Have you sent out the invites?"

"Yep." I tuck my hands in my back pockets and do a final turn through the building, double-checking where we placed the weapons. I sent Leo, Thom, and Chris invitations from The Dollhouse website. Knowing their predilections, I crafted an enticing summons they wouldn't be able to refuse.

Sinister comes up behind me and wraps an arm around my waist. "Ready?" At my nod, he flips the switch, and the blue lights come on. I turn in a slow circle, taking everything in. On the retractable wall to the third section, he drew a monster and a wren. Another wall holds our names and the date they separated us. Scythes, crosses, and other deathly images cover the remaining walls, along with my original words that he's interspersed with the pictures.

"It's perfect," I breathe, and Sin grins down at me. "Now let's get ready. They'll be here soon."

CHAPTER TEN

SINISTER

D olly spins around and throws her arms out. "What do you think?" She's wearing one of the new dresses I bought her, a pale-pink one with a lot of flounces and lace. Frilly socks and her Mary Janes complete her outfit, and she's styled her hair into two French braids intertwined with pink ribbons.

I dressed myself in my usual Carver attire. Black slacks, brogues, a white button-down shirt, and a trench coat that flows down to my knees. I modified it to add hidden pockets to store a variety of weapons.

"Perfect," I reply, dropping a kiss on her forehead. An alert pings my phone, letting me know there's movement out front. Dolly's head snaps up, and a smile spreads across her face. She's adorable.

She grabs my hand, and we hurry down the stairs. I close the wall behind us as Dolly heads to the front to let Chris in. She staggered their arrival times so they wouldn't be suspicious when they saw each other. I tuck myself behind the door and give her a nod. She winks back and pulls the door open, and I notice the change in her behavior immediately.

"Welcome to The Dollhouse, sir. Please, come on in," she

says in a sensual voice, grabbing his arm and pulling him inside. "Here, let me take your coat." While he's distracted, I come up behind him and plunge a needle into his neck. His hand comes up to cover the injection site, and he spins around, backing up when he catches sight of me.

"Wha—" He collapses to the ground, his eyes rolling up into his head. The corner of my mouth ticks up. It's another of The Chemist's formulas. The fast-acting concoction knocks them out and loosens their muscles, allowing for easy transport.

Dolly bounces on her toes. "You're going to introduce The Chemist to me, right? I need to meet this man."

I growl low in my throat and wrap a hand around her neck. "Mine." My lips capture hers, and my tongue plunders her mouth. "Don't get any ideas," I say after leaving her weaving on her feet.

She blinks at me before turning with a huff. "I'll have ideas if I want to." She lifts Chris's legs and raises a brow at me. "Going to help me, or do I have to do everything by myself?"

"Dolly."

She scowls back. "What?"

"Dolly."

She drops his legs and places her hands on her hips. "Spit it out, Carver. I don't have all day. Thom's going to be here in ten minutes."

"That's enough time," I say, advancing toward her.

She audibly gulps and takes a step back. "Time for what?"

I grab her arm and force her to her knees. "To teach that bratty mouth a lesson. Don't think I don't know when you're trying to provoke me. If you want your brother's cock, all you have to do is ask." I unzip my pants and pull my cock out. It got hard the second she began mouthing off, and she licks her lips and opens her mouth like the good little sister she is.

My cock slides into her warm, wet mouth, and as much as I'd like to take my time, it won't be long before Thom knocks on the door. I place my hands on her cheeks and hold her still. Her eyes widen when I slide to the back of her throat, making her gag.

Fuck.

"That's it, little stalker. Now suck." Drool drips from her chin, puddling on the concrete floor. "Don't you dare," I warn when she dips her hand beneath her dress. "Your orgasms are mine, and you haven't earned one yet."

Dolly groans around my cock and glares up at me with narrowed eyes. Still sassy. I'll never tell her how much I secretly enjoy it.

My hands tighten along with my balls, and I snap my hips forward, driving my cock farther down her throat. "Good girl," I murmur. "Fuck, you're so beautiful with your mouth wrapped around me." My head jerks back as my orgasm hits me, and I pour my release down her throat.

Cum dribbles from her mouth as I withdraw, and I reach down to push it back in. "Don't waste any, little sister. Swallow it all down." Dolly bites the pad of my thumb, making me hiss. She climbs to her feet and flounces off, leaving behind the scent of her arousal. She's going to be the death of me, but I can't think of a better way to go.

After tucking myself away, I stride over to where I dumped Chris's body. Dolly hums under her breath while she watches me pull his clothes off and strap his arms to a four-foot horizontal pole. Once he's secured, Dolly flicks a switch on a remote control, setting the pulley into motion. Chains clink and rattle as he's lifted into the air, his body banging against the metal wall. The pulley locks into place, securing him about fifteen feet up.

We repeat the process—sans blowjob—when Thom arrives, and again for Leo. Dolly switches the lights off, and we wait in the dark for the men to wake. A grin splits my face when their chains rattle and they cry out in fear.

Now they'll know how we felt.

I click on the blue lights, and one of them shouts. The other two look around wildly, their heads turning as they take in the pictures and words painted on the walls.

"Now you have no one," Dolly calls out, her clear voice echoing throughout the building as she repeats the words they used fourteen years ago. "No one will save you. No one is coming for you."

"We shoulda killed you that day," Leo shouts, his heels kicking against the wall.

"Yes, you should have," she replies. "You should have put a stake through my heart. You should have burned my body and spread the ashes to the winds. Instead, you sold a child into slavery, and I'm here to collect my dues."

We lower Leo, and the second he's within arm's reach, I inject him with the serum I used on Jack. He flails against the chains as it takes effect, and even in the shadows, I see the pulse in his neck speed up. I jerk my head at Dolly, and the corner of her mouth lifts as she steps back. After unclipping Leo, I clap a hand on his shoulder, holding him steady.

"You have fifteen minutes. If you make it through the maze, you can leave here with your life," I explain, pointing toward the entrance. "We'll even let your buddies help you. They can guide you through it."

A scoreboard along the middle wall lowers with a shrill screech reminiscent of nails on a chalkboard. The number fifteen lights up, and three loud blasts sound as the number flashes.

Dolly disappeared into the tunnels when the blasts went off, and when the clock begins to count down, I push Leo away. "Better hurry now," I say before jogging away. There's no need to stand back and watch—he does exactly what I knew he would. With his body flooded with adrenaline and mind consumed with fear, he went straight to the nearest exit.

I roll my eyes as I duck into the farthest tunnel and scoop up a scythe. The idiot will waste several minutes of his time pounding against the door we barricaded and locked with chains after his arrival. Once he realizes he can't get out, he'll either have a tantrum, give up and refuse to move, or enter the maze.

The stupid fucking bastard wasted seven minutes. Chris and Thom spent the first three yelling at him to get into the maze, but he was too pigheaded to listen. I watch out of the peepholes as he comes to a stop in front of the entrance, his chest heaving with deep breaths.

Finally.

His fists curl and he takes a giant step inside, then freezes as he waits for something to happen. When nothing does, he takes a tentative step forward, and then another. Dolly pushes a hidden panel closed from inside the tunnel, blocking the entrance. He jumps, glances behind him, and takes off, choosing the left passage.

"Right!" Chris shouts. "Go right at the next junction."

Leo turns onto the path where I'm hiding. His shadow falls over the ground, and I drop to my knees, swing my arm back, and slide the scythe under the gap. Leo's high-pitched scream punches into the silent room as he falls on his ass, clutching his ankle. When I see the blood spurting from the deep wound, I huff a laugh.

"Georgie Porgie, pudding and pie. Kissed the girls and made them cry," Dolly chants, her voice clear over the shouts.

"What the fuck?" Leo says, his voice wobbling like a child.

"Now that wasn't very nice of Georgie," Dolly states, materializing out of the wall like a ghost. She swings her bat in the air before pointing it at him. "You shouldn't make girls cry."

Barbie connects with Leo's knee, shattering it. His terrified scream pierces the air, and Chris and Thom shout back, rattling their chains. Dolly ducks back into the tunnel, and Leo shouts, "I'm going to fucking kill you, you little bitch." He hauls himself to his feet and limps down the path.

Thom shouts directions, and we let him advance a bit before Dolly starts again. *"When the boys came out to play..."* That's my cue.

I step out in front of him and cock my head, letting him see the monster inside me. *"Georgie Porgie ran away,"* I finish for her in a steely voice. Leo rears back and trips over his feet, landing on his ass with a grunt.

I drop to my haunches and stare at him. "You hurt my sister. You took her away from me and forced her to witness my death. And then what did you do, Leo?" My knife slides out of my coat sleeve, and I spin it between my fingers. When he refuses to answer, I strike down and scrape the knife against the concrete floor between his legs.

"What did you do, Leo?" I ask again softly. "No? Don't want to admit what you did to a terrorized eight-year-old? Hmm?" I jump to my feet, walk behind him, and grab hold of his hair, yanking his head back.

Dolly skips toward me, her eyes twinkling with glee. I think I love this woman. Whoa. Fuck. I'll have to come back to that thought later. When she reaches us, she slides a ten-inch dildo from behind her back.

"Be a good boy and suck this dick," she says, forcing it into his mouth. He struggles against my hold, but I keep a firm grip on him. "Look, Sinister. I think he likes it. I bet he wants more." She pulls it back before ramming it farther down his throat. His back arches, his hands slapping at the air as she pushes it even farther.

His eyes bulge, mirroring his throat, and he stares up at me like I might save him. "Leo, Leo," I murmur as a wicked smile spreads across my face. "Did you really think we'd let any of you walk out of here alive?"

Dolly chuckles and pinches his nose shut with one hand while forcing him to swallow another inch of the dildo. "Of course not. But we had to at least give them hope now, didn't we?" Leo's shoulders drop and tears leak from his eyes. He doesn't stop looking at me, and I'm glad I'm the last thing he'll see.

I was forced to see his face a thousand times in my nightmares.

When his eyes glaze over, I drop him like the trash he is and haul Dolly into my arms. She winds her hands into my hair and meets my mouth with hers. Thom and Chris shout and rattle, but we ignore them.

"Three down, little bird. Three to go."

CHAPTER ELEVEN

DOLLY

My heart races as I dash back into the tunnels while Sinister sets Thom free and restarts the clock. He's smarter than Leo; he races into the maze while Chris shouts instructions to him. I let him get further in before sliding the entrance panel shut and heading toward the middle.

Chris, from his vantage point, may be able to view ninety percent of the maze, but he can't see the exit—because there isn't one. His help will only send Thom into a dead end, where we'll be waiting for him.

A shiver of glee runs over my shoulders at the knowledge that they get to experience some of the fear we did. Watching their friends die, knowing they're helpless to do anything to stop it, and realizing they're next. The hope of an escape followed by the certainty of death.

Fuck them and what they put us through. They deserve this, and I'm glad I'm fucked up enough to not feel guilty over not feeling guilty. The world will be a better place without them.

I stop at the next peephole and wait for Thom to pass by. After closing off this section, I follow him toward the center, palming my knife. A list of potential nursery rhymes plays through my mind, and a smile flutters at my lips as I select the perfect one.

"Three blind mice, three blind mice. See how they run, see how they run..."

"Fuck off, you freaky bitch!" Thom shouts, making me chuckle. Sinister won't like that.

"They all ran after the farmer's wife..." I slide out from behind the wall, appearing in front of him. He shouts and stumbles backward, right into Sinister's chest. I tilt my head and slash the knife through the air. *"She cut off their tails with a carving knife."*

"No! No, fuck you." Sinister wraps his arms around Thom's, holding him in place. His face grows red as I advance, and he fights against Sinister's superior grip. I raise my arm but stop and look at my brother with a raised brow. His lips purse, but he nods.

Thom's legs scramble against the floor, the whites of his eyes showing as I snap gloves on. I'm not touching that with my bare skin. Once was enough for a lifetime.

"Did you ever see such a sight in your life..." I sing, drawing out the words in a lower octave. My hand whips out and grabs his dick, stretching it toward me. *"As three blind mice."*

Thoms neck bulges as screams rip from his throat. Poor guy. I should have chosen a sharper knife. Blood spurts everywhere, staining my dress as the air fills with the coppery scent. I end up having to use a sawing motion to cut off the offending member Thom used to harm so many children.

Now, he'll never be able to hurt anyone again.

"You know, you're awfully loud," I remark, waving his severed penis in the air like a trophy. "Good little boys keep their mouths shut. Sin, could you help me out?"

Sinister forces Thom to his knees and squeezes the sides of his jaw, making him open his mouth. Thom glares at me, his eyes filled with hatred. I giggle and stuff his dick in his mouth, pressing it down into his throat. Sin snaps Thom's chin up and holds his mouth closed.

"You know, I don't like the way he's looking at me, Sin. Maybe he should be as blind as the mice too." Thom tries to shake his head, but Sinister's hands tighten their grip on him. Knowing the serum Sin gave him won't allow him to lose consciousness makes this all the better.

I don't have long before he suffocates on his dick, though, so I work fast, slashing an X over each eye. Gurgled noises sound in his throat, and his whole body trembles before he gives up the fight. Sinister releases his body and steps over him, pulling me into his side. He drops a kiss on my forehead and whispers, "Four down, little bird."

After resetting the clock and pulling the panels back, I tap my brother on the shoulder. "Sin, I'm bored. This maze thing just isn't doing it for me. Can we switch it up a little?"

"Read my mind, little stalker." Sinister strides over to a panel and switches off the blue lights and scoreboard. The warehouse plunges into darkness, and Chris cuts off his endless complaints. Thank fuck.

Strobe lights click on, blue and purple pulses of light that illuminate then shadow the room. The demonic and eerie notes of Khanate's "Commuted" fill the room, causing a sliver of apprehension to slither down my spine.

Chris struggles in his chains as his body lowers down the wall, and he kicks out at Sinister when he walks toward him with a syringe in his hand. Sinister punches him in the face and injects it before grabbing his chin. "I can end this now. Tell me where Richard Norris is, and I'll kill you quickly. No torture, no pain."

Chris sobs and shakes his head. "I don't know," he blubbers. "Last I heard, he was in Chicago. He left Arcadia years ago."

Sinister cocks his head and tuts. "Well, now, that's a shame." He unclips Chris's hands and shoves him away. "I suggest you start running." I lick my lips and lean down to pick up Barbie. She hasn't seen enough action today and deserves to wet her thirst. Chris stumbles away, then turns and runs around the side of the maze.

Sinister and I exchange glances. He jerks his head toward Chris's pasty naked ass disappearing around the corner. "Ladies first."

I laugh and drop a curtsy. "Thank you, kind sir." The music sets fire to my blood, and the anticipation of the hunt sets my feet in motion. Barbie swings back and forth as I stalk my prey, humming along with the song as I go. Glancing over my shoulder, I notice Sinister ducking into a tunnel.

That man is perfect for me. He accepts me just as I am, both Wren and Dolly. He makes me feel things other than anger and has given me back parts of myself I thought were lost. The thought of spending forever at his side both thrills and terrifies me. He's wormed his way into my heart, blowing apart my defenses and setting up home there.

I wouldn't survive his loss. Not a second time.

Up ahead, the strobe lights flash over Chris's huddled body as he peers around the corner of the maze. I bite my lip to keep from laughing and tiptoe up behind him. Barbie slashes through the air, her blades twinkling blue and purple as she lands at the base of his spine, tearing into his flesh and making it rain blood.

I dance away and push through a hidden door into the tunnels, leaving Chris howling behind. A hand wraps around my mouth, and I'm yanked against a hard chest. "You're so fucking perfect, little stalker. Watching you spill blood makes my dick hard." A shiver runs down my body when he takes Barbie from my hand and drops her to the floor. He flips my dress up with one hand, while the other moves off my mouth and cups my neck.

He pushes inside me with a hard thrust, making me moan. "Fuck me like you mean it, Sin." He chuckles and pushes my back down before fucking me so hard my teeth rattle. I reach out to hold on to the wall, my body jerking with each thrust. "You better make me come this time."

"Do you think you've earned it?"

"Yes?"

His hand tightens around my throat, and he pulls back before slamming into me. "Touch your clit and make yourself come while I fuck this pretty pussy," he says, and I waste no time obeying. He left me wet and unsatisfied earlier, so I'm not risking him changing his mind.

I slide my hand under my dress and fondle his balls, making him curse. I giggle and move up to my clit, soft moans spilling from my lips as I circle the small bud.

"That's it, baby. Fuck, I can feel your walls clenching around me. So fucking good." I clamp down around him and shout his name as I come. "Yes, yes, yes," he hisses. His hand tightens more around my neck, cutting off my air flow as he stills, coming deep inside me.

He pulls me up and bites into the base of my neck. Not hard enough to break the skin, but enough to leave a mark. He pulls out of me with an obscenely wet noise and runs a hand over the bite mark.

"I'm going to tattoo this into your skin so everyone knows you're mine," he says before flipping my dress down.

I spin around, lean up on my toes, and press a kiss to the corner of his mouth. "Or, you could use a more traditional method," I say.

He raises a brow. "What would that be?"

"You could put a ring on it," I reply, scooping up Barbie and skipping away. Sinister barks a laugh, but I ignore him and keep going. Chris is waiting, and it's time to put him out of his misery.

Stalking through the warehouse, my head swivels back and forth as I hunt for my prey. The music switches to Haxan

Cloak's "Mist," the dark base and eerie yips driving me forward.

Chris dives from behind a wall and rams into me, knocking me down. "Die, cunt," he grits out, kicking me in the side. But I'm not unfamiliar with pain and abuse, so I brush it off and crab-crawl backward, dragging Barbie with me.

"You just fucked up," I say as I pull myself to my feet. "My brother doesn't like it when other men touch me."

"He's a sick fuck," Chris spits, running a hand over his mouth. "At least when I made you suck me, I wasn't your brother." His hand trembles and his eyes widen. "I'm sorry, I didn't—" A low growl cuts him off, and he shivers at the sound.

My head snaps to the right, my heart thumping like a caged animal when Sinister steps out of the shadows. A blue flash of light illuminates the snarl on his face before it moves away. He moves silently up behind me, towering over me, a furious megalith of destruction.

Chris backs up, raising his hands in supplication when Sinister steps around me, scraping his scythe along the floor. Bright sparks ignite along the edge, and I watch in fascination as the man who's come to mean everything to me takes Chris's head off in one fell swoop. It lands on the floor with a gruesome plop, its mouth opening and closing before it freezes in place. The body crashes to the floor, blood spilling out and covering it with a crimson stain.

I drop Barbie and throw myself into Sin's arms, wrapping my arms around his neck. He holds me close and whispers his mantra. "Five down, little bird. One to go."

I squeeze him tighter and reply, "I seem to remember what you said would happen if another man touched me."

Sinister throws his head back and laughs before setting me down and sealing my mouth with his. "Goddamn, woman. I love you."

CHAPTER TWELVE

WREN

Three Weeks Later

I tap my fingers on the windowsill, staring blankly out of the window as the bus ambles along Arcadia's streets. "Come on, come on," I murmur as panic mounts inside me. Something's wrong. Very wrong.

Sinister went out the night before last to do one of his walks through downtown. He likes to keep his eye on "his city," as he calls it. But he didn't come home. At first, I thought little of it. After all, he has things to do and Aidan's business to help run. But as the hours ticked by with no word, I began to worry.

Maybe I'm paranoid. Perhaps Aidan's taken a turn for the worse, or Sin got caught up with work. But if there's one thing he takes seriously, it's his word. He kissed me goodbye and told me he'd be back that night.

Only he never showed. And his cell phone goes to voicemail every time I call it.

A lump forms in my throat at the thought of something

happening to him. My hands tremble, and I clasp them together, my knuckles turning white. I can't think like that. He's fine. Maybe Aidan needed him to torture someone, and he's lost track of time.

Please let that be it.

I press the bell and jump out of the seat, working my way to the front. My foot taps impatiently as the driver slows to a stop. I barely wait for the doors to swoosh open before catapulting myself out of them and onto the busy sidewalk. Aidan's compound lies three blocks to the west, and my feet automatically turn that way, breaking into a run and shouting at people to get out of the way.

The ten-foot iron gates loom before me, and I stop at the booth to tell the guard my name. Only, there is no guard. My chest heaves as I suck in air, fighting the swelling panic. Sinister told me a guard is always on duty, so where is he?

The metal handrail creaks as I pull myself up the steep stairs and peer through the window. The blood-splattered window. Jesus fucking Christ. A man lies on the floor of the small booth, his chest riddled with bullets.

My mouth dries as I clamber down the stairs and walk over to the gates. Whoever killed the guard didn't close them all the way. I push against one, straining to force it to open just enough for me to slip through. Ahead of me is a quarter-of-a-mile winding driveway, surrounded by green lawns and lined with trees. The compound rises three stories at the end of it, with two lookout towers at each side.

Fuck. Fuck, fuck, fuck! Every part of me wants to run forward and burst inside. I know Sinister's in there. I just do. But there's only one of me, and besides the couple of knives I've tucked into my pockets, I'm not armed.

And I can't walk into a gunfight with a knife.

Indecision locks me in place. What the fuck do I do? *Breathe, Wren.*

I slip back out of the gate and lean against the wall

surrounding the compound. There's no way I can do this alone. There's no telling how many people are inside, if any. If anyone is alive. If Sin...No. Just no.

I pull my phone out of my pocket and click on the bloody kiss. "Pick up. Please, pick up." The screen clears, and I almost cry with relief. "Hello?"

One heartbeat, two heartbeats, three.

"Dolly? What's wrong?" Cruz, Dutch's husband, asks. He moves into the frame and sits down. I can't help it. Tears mist my eyes before sliding down my cheeks. Asking for help isn't something I'm comfortable with, but I need it now, and I can't let past traumas prevent me from doing what I need to.

"Cruz, I need help. Please. Something's happened to Sinister." I explain about the dead guard and my intuition telling me he's in trouble. "I don't have adequate weapons, and I need back-up. Are you guys still in Australia?"

Cruz nods. "Yeah, we'll be here for some time yet." His brows furrow, and he turns his head to the left. "Trey, do you know where The Duke is?" he calls out. "Just a minute, Dolly." He gets up and moves off screen.

My back slides down the wall, and I land in the soft grass. Minutes tick by, and with each one, my anxiety ramps up further. I pound my fist on my thigh and blow out breaths, willing myself to calm down. Sinister needs me to be functional, not a blubbering mess. If he saw me right now, he'd be disappointed in me.

That thought makes me sit up straighter and dash away the tears. I survived my parents' deaths. The loss of my home. The supposed death of my brother. I lived through countless assaults, torture, and starvation.

I can get through this.

Cruz comes back onto the screen and gives me a smile. "You're in luck. The Duke is about an hour away with her team. Trey pinged your location and sent it to her. Don't worry, help is on the way. Sit tight, okay? The girls send their love."

"Thank you," I say. "If we can ever return the favor—"

"We'll let you know. Good luck, Dolly." The screen goes blank, and I tuck the phone back in my pocket. All I can do now is wait.

~

I HEAR them before I see them. A dark-gray helicopter appears in the distance, and I head back through the gates and stand on the grass, covering my eyes with my hand as it comes closer. The force of the wind makes me brace, the vibrations running through me and making me tremble.

It lands about two hundred feet from me, and once the blades stop whirring, a woman jumps out of the front and strides toward me. She has long blonde hair and wears all-black military-style clothing. A coiled whip wraps around her shoulder, and she walks like a fucking boss.

I nearly snap to attention and salute her. Thank God I stop myself at the last second.

Six men tumble out of the back of the helicopter and join us. They, too, are dressed all in black, and I'm relieved to see them packing guns, knives, and what looks like gas canisters.

"Dolly? I'm The Duke. I hear you're in need of help. Can you tell me the situation?"

"I don't know. My...boyfriend, Sinister, has been missing for almost two days. His phone goes straight to voicemail, and when I arrived here, I found the guard dead at his post." I point toward the gate. "Oh, and the gate was left open. I can't say for sure he's inside, or if he is, who else is in there. I-I don't even know if he's alive," I finish with a whisper.

"How was the guard killed?"

"Gun."

"Do you know how many people are normally inside?" I

shake my head. It wasn't something we had discussed, and I hadn't been inside the compound often enough to notice.

The Duke taps her hand against her thigh and blows out a breath. "Okay, I want two of you around the back, one at each side, and two at the front. Mask up, vest up. There are possible civilians inside, so we'll use the gas and rubber bullets. Dolly, you'll be with me." She leads us back to the helicopter, where I'm fitted with a bulletproof vest, thigh pads, and a gas mask.

"Do you know how to use a gun?" The Duke asks.

"No, I'm more of a knife kind of girl."

"Ah, you're like Tessa and Rebecca, then. Here." She hands me two military knives and helps me strap them to my vest. "All right, boys, there's nothing stealthy about this. No one inside that building missed the sound of the copter touching down. Let's do this."

As one, we race across the lawn. Prickles of sweat dot my brow, and I can't help but feel a surge of hope. If Sinister's alive, we're going to get him out.

When we near the compound, our group splits up according to The Duke's instructions. We pull our masks on and run up the stairs, exchanging looks at the wide-open doors. One man stops at the threshold and throws a canister in. It slides across the floor, emitting a cloud of gas.

We step inside, but the foyer is suspiciously quiet. No one is at the reception desk, but the walls are covered in dried-blood splatter. *Fuck.* What the hell happened here? The Duke points two fingers, and the two men with us split off, one going right, one left.

"Where are Sinister's rooms?" she asks, her voice muffled by her mask. I gesture toward the stairs, and The Duke pushes me behind her and heads up first, gun trained and sweeping back and forth. Once we hit the landing, I'm again astonished at the silence. At least there's no blood up here.

We take our masks off and attach them to our vests. The Duke pulls to a stop and presses a finger to her ear. "Got it," she replies. "Dolly, they found people locked in the basement. Eight dead, seventeen alive. Sinister wasn't among them."

I give a jerky nod and fist my trembling hands. *Stay calm. Breathe.*

The Duke sweeps each room we pass but appears to let her guard down when they continue to turn up empty. I pull to a stop outside Aidan's room, a slither of premonition locking my muscles. My head shakes back and forth, then I squeeze my eyes closed and push the door open.

My knees give out, and I fall to the floor, gasping for air. The nurse lies sprawled on the floor with a bullet in her head. And Aidan...fuck. His sightless eyes stare at the ceiling, while the jagged slash in his neck mocks me with a crimson grin.

The Duke grabs my arm and hauls me to my feet. I stumble into the room, coming to a stop by his bed. I take his icy hand in mine and whisper, "Go in peace, Aidan. Thank you for keeping him safe for me."

Shock and sorrow morph into anger, and my chest burns with the need for blood. Whoever did this is a dead man. And if they hurt Sinister, I'm going to make it as painful as possible.

I storm out of the room and head toward Sinister's apartment, pulling out the knives as I go. The Duke follows me silently, keeping her own counsel. *Calm down. Don't lose it. Stay alert.* Fuck that.

I hurl myself at his door and tumble through it like the Tasmanian Devil on steroids. The living room is empty, so I carry on toward the bedroom. The moment I enter the hallway, I see him through the open door. Someone strapped him to his bed, gagged him, and he sports shallow-looking slashes all over his bare chest.

The Duke tries to grab my arm, but I shake her off and race toward the room. Sinister's eyes widen, and he screams into the gag, shaking his head. He struggles against the bonds, the muscles in his arms standing in relief. It's enough to warn me when a shadow appears from behind the door.

Richard steps out from behind it with his gun raised and pointed at my head. "Well, well, well. If it isn't the little bird, alive and well. I have to say, I was surprised to discover you were still alive." I freeze in place as childhood memories slam into me with the force of a tidal wave. My teeth clench as I force them back into their box. I don't have the luxury of spiraling.

"That both of you are still alive," he goes on. "So imagine my surprise when I got word of Jack's and Evan's deaths, followed by Chris's, Leo's, and Thom's disappearance. You two have been busy, haven't you?"

"We have," I agree. A smile lifts the corners of my mouth. "All to draw you out, of course. Thank you for making it easy for us."

Richard's features twist with unease, and I take that moment to drop to the ground. The Duke steps forward and shoots him in the leg but not with one of her rubber bullets. His knee explodes in a shower of blood, and he drops his gun when he crashes to the floor with an ear-piercing scream. The Duke steps over me and kicks the gun away before heading toward Sinister.

"You can take the trash out," she says, tossing me a grin.

I crawl to my knees and straddle Richard's waist, placing one knife to his throat. "Who do you work for?"

He sneers at me, even as he writhes in pain. "Go fuck yourself, you little cunt." My arm whips out, and I stab it through his hand, pinning him to the wooden floor. His back arches beneath me, trying to buck me off him as he lets out a pained shout.

"Who do you work for?" I scream back at him, pressing the other knife tighter against his throat. A slick line of blood appears, and Richard's eyes bulge.

"Governor White," he grits out, baring his teeth at me.

"He'll roast you both alive. He's better guarded than Fort Knox—you don't stand a chance against him." The last of his words come out gargled as I plunge the knife into his chest. Years of suffering and hatred pour out of me as my arm swings down over and over again. Hot metallic blood splatters my face and obscures my vision, while tears stream down my cheeks and pool on his chest.

Time ceases to exist as I exorcise my demons on the man responsible for it all. His heart stops beating long before I'm satisfied, and I only stop when Sinister pulls me off him and wraps his arms around me.

I sob into his shoulder, hot desperate tears of relief. He's okay. He's alive. The pain in my chest eases as he whispers in my ear. "It's okay. Shh, Wren. Sinister is here, and no one will hurt you again. You're safe."

EPILOGUE
SINISTER

One Month Later

I lean on my elbow, staring down at Wren. My hand runs up and down her back, soothing her while she sleeps. I'll never forget the way she looked the day she came to rescue me, all fierce and murderous.

It still irks me that Richard got the jump on me, but he came with a team of men that he dismissed after he took the compound. My chest aches with the memory of Aidan's passing, but it may have been a blessing in disguise. I wish he hadn't suffered such a violent death, but it was a quicker and perhaps more merciful one than the one that awaited him.

Wren shifts and mumbles under her breath before burrowing into my chest. She's the lone light in the dark, the whole reason I continue to breathe. She's stood by me every step of the way—planning and executing Aidan's funeral, cementing my place as the head of his organization, and coming up with plans for our future.

Because, let's face it, there is no future without her.

～

WE STAND OUTSIDE the door leading to the restaurant's kitchen with our backs pressed against the wall. Inside, chefs bustle about, finishing the five-course meal for the group of eighteen men gathered inside. They booked the entire restaurant for their party, and their obnoxious laughter rises above the clatter of pots and pans.

I lean over Wren and place a staccato of knocks on the door. Moments later, the five chefs exit with their heads turned down and file into a waiting bus. Carlos, after surviving the attack on the compound, wanted in on our little adventure, and offered to drive the chefs home.

Wren and I slip inside, the scent of spices and cooking meat assaulting our senses. I pull out the glass bottle The Chemist gave me. Inside is an odorless, tasteless poison that induces terrifying hallucinations, followed by bleeding from the eyes, nose, and ears. As it works through your system, it destroys your veins and melts your organs, leading to an agonizing death within twenty minutes of digesting it.

I add it to every dish, and for good measure, dump some into the water pitchers too. When I'm done, I signal for the seven waiters to come in. The Duke allowed us to borrow some of her men, who were all on board with dressing up in tuxedos and moonlighting at waiters.

Six of them disappear into the restaurant with their trays of food and water, while the seventh slips around to the front and bolts the doors with heavy chains. Once they're served, we leave out the back and secure those doors as well.

Wren whoops and does a little happy dance before flinging herself at me. "We did it."

I chuckle and bop her on the nose. "We did. Want to

watch?" She scoffs and grabs my hand, entwining our fingers. We take a leisurely stroll around the outside of the building, coming to a stop at the front where large picture windows dominate the walls.

Governor White stands in front of the table with a glass in his hand as he gives a toast. The seated men raise theirs in return—some of whom were frequent visitors at Grammy Lockwood's Home For Girls.

We watch as they spoon their poisoned soup into their mouths, and it isn't long before the first sign appears. A man throws himself out of his chair, his mouth open on a scream, pointing at the opposite wall.

The hallucinations have begun.

One man punches another, while one huddles on the floor, rocking back and forth. Governor White falls off his chair, clutching his chest. Wren watches with wide-eyed wonder, squeezing my fingers so hard, she cuts off the circulation.

I spin her around before dipping her and kissing her deeply. The windows behind us rattle with the fists of the men pounding against it. When I straighten her, Wren's pupils are dilated, and her chest heaves to catch her breath.

My arm slides down hers, and I take her hand in mine. She glances down, puzzled, her eyes widening when I slip the black diamond ring on her finger. Her head snaps up, her eyes filled with tears as her gaze searches mine.

My throat tightens. I have a hundred things I could say. *You are my world. My heart. My everything. Stay by my side and be my queen.*

Instead, all that pops out is, "Well, you told me to put a ring on it."

A broken sob spills from her mouth. With the cacophony of screams in the background playing our song, she lifts her mouth to mine and seals our fates with a kiss.

~

Want to learn more about Dolly's guardian angels? Make sure to check out the Vengeance Series!

ABOUT THE AUTHOR

A former American, Michaella now calls Scotland home. When she isn't discreetly checking out men in kilts or chasing the wild haggis through the glens, you can usually find her skulking about the online bookish community.

Michaella has always been fascinated with the darker, more macabre facets of the human psyche and doesn't shy away from controversial, taboo, and dark themes in her writing.

A self-proclaimed book nerd, she's happiest curled up on the sofa with a good book and a margarita or two, while merrily adding more book boyfriends to her already over-flowing harem.

Made in the USA
Middletown, DE
18 August 2024

59368945R00055